W9-BAI-473

STILL WATERS

*Also by Jill Giencke
in Large Print:*

Secrets of Echo Moon
Fatal Facts

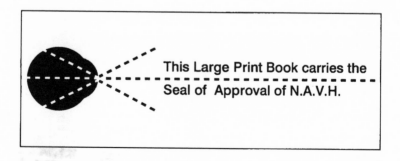

STILL WATERS

■

JILL GIENCKE

-t
f
GIE

Thorndike Press • Thorndike, Maine

Library of Congress Cataloging in Publication Data

Giencke, Jill, 1959–
    Still waters / Jill Giencke.
        p.   cm.
    ISBN 0-7862-1738-3 (lg. print : hc : alk. paper)
    1. Large type books. I. Title.
    [PS3557.I258S74 1999]
    813'.54—dc21   98-48767

To Pam and Alex and Joseph
With love from Aunt Jill

Chapter One

"*Oakwood Herald.* Lauren Sterling speaking." I'd snatched up the phone on the first ring. It was three o'clock in the afternoon. Two hours until deadline and my story on the school-board meeting the night before was still just notes on a page. The last thing I needed was an interruption, but here it was.

"Just the person I was hoping for." The voice on the line was only vaguely familiar. Male, low, and husky. A pleasant voice, I decided.

"How can I help you?" I prodded.

"This is Alderman Whitson. Ross Whitson. I need to talk to you. Preferably as soon as possible."

Ross Whitson. My brain shifted rapidly through a catalog of local officials. His face sprang readily to mind, and with good reason. There were those who said he'd been elected on his looks alone.

"May I ask why, sir?"

There was hesitation and I heard some

papers rattling around. He sighed and spoke. "I know this sounds melodramatic, Miss Sterling, but I'd rather not discuss it over the phone."

I frowned. It certainly did sound odd. Rolling my eyes, I pulled my calendar closer so I could check my schedule. "Okay. How about tomorrow at two?" I suggested, reaching up behind my ear for the pencil that usually sat there.

"That should be fine. I'll pick you up at your office," he said.

"Are we going somewhere?"

"Just for a drive," Whitson said mysteriously. "See you then. And thank you."

After I hung up, I allowed myself a few seconds to wonder what the call had been about. "Starting to run for reelection awfully early," I muttered aloud. The school-board story beckoned and I turned to my computer. There'd be time for Mr. Whitson tomorrow. Now I had a deadline to meet.

The next day, I was ready and waiting just before two. The *Herald* is Oakwood's only newspaper, and has appeared regularly each Thursday since the turn of the century. Since it is printed on Wednesdays, those are usually quiet days at the office, all the action being in the pressroom. Today was no exception. Only two or three other reporters sat at their desks, answering phones or already working on stories for next week's issue.

Picking up my coffee mug — a huge ceramic affair bearing the words *I brake for chocolate* — I drank the last ice-cold sip and grimaced. I hoped Mr. Whitson planned to take me to lunch.

Peering into the tiny mirror of my compact, I brushed powder onto my nose and added another stroke of lipstick to my lips. Dark-blue eyeliner deepened the blue of my eyes; a touch of blush brought more color to my cheeks. Whisking a brush through my short brown hair made it fluff gently around my face. Done!

I gathered up my purse and my notebook and went down to the office lobby. Might as well meet him at the door, I figured. Outside, a light snow was falling. Here in the Midwest, snow in March is expected, if not anxiously anticipated. I was glad I'd worn a sweater and heavy corduroy skirt. As I reached for my coat, the bell above the door gave a jingle and a draft of cold air blew in. The receptionist called out a greeting and I turned to meet my two o'clock appointment.

Ross Whitson stood just inside the door, wearing a heavy winter coat and a politician's smile. He was tall, about six foot two, I guessed. His dark hair was dusted with snowflakes and he smiled as he brushed them away.

"You're Lauren Sterling," he stated, stepping forward and extending a hand.

I smiled and gave it a shake. "Yes, I am. You're Alderman Whitson."

He flinched, closing his eyes in a grimace that still couldn't mar his boyish good looks. "Please, call me Ross. That 'alderman' stuff makes me feel like I should be eighty years old."

"All right. Ross, then." He was nowhere near eighty, of course. I knew because that morning I'd made a trip to the paper's morgue and looked up some background information. I knew he was thirty-four. The youngest alderman Oakwood had seen in years, he'd been elected easily over his opponent, the incumbent. He had a small but successful law practice here in town, having returned after several years of seeing the world.

"Shall we?" He gestured toward the door and held it for me, then led the way to his car, a late-model automobile that was neither sporty nor grand. A functional family car, it seemed an odd choice for a bachelor such as Ross. Still, it gleamed a sparkling silver in the wintery sunshine and soon Ross had turned onto the highway headed out of town.

For the first few minutes, neither of us spoke and I began to wonder when he'd tell me whatever it was that was bothering him.

"Thank you for agreeing to meet me, Lauren," he said, darting a glance my way while his hands remained steady on the wheel. "I realize my call must have sounded like the opening scene of an old movie, so I'm glad you took me seriously."

I laughed and pulled my gloves farther over my wrists. "Truthfully, Ross, I'm not taking you seriously yet. You haven't told me anything."

"That's true, I guess." He didn't seem bothered by my honesty, and went on. "Okay, here it is. I've become aware of a major problem in Oakwood." His tone was serious and his face grave as he continued. "One that could have catastrophic consequences if it isn't stopped immediately. I want you to expose it in the *Herald.* Bring the criminal to justice."

I blinked. This certainly wasn't what I'd expected. "Excuse me. Which criminal? What's the crime?" As I spoke, I fished my notebook from my purse and uncapped my pen.

"I'm not sure who the criminal really is, Lauren. That's part of what I need you to find out."

11

"Maybe you should be talking to a detective. I'm just a reporter, you know," I pointed out.

"Not 'just a reporter,' " he corrected me. "I've been reading your stories ever since I came back to Oakwood. You're a fine writer, with a keen eye. You ask the right questions, and that's why I need you."

I sighed, partly in confusion, mostly in resignation. "Why don't you tell me what you do know — the whole story — and I'll see what I can do. You've certainly piqued my curiosity."

He smiled and I could see why he was so popular with the townspeople. He'd gotten more than his fair share of charm. The smile he beamed at me could have powered Oakwood for a week. For just an instant, I forgot why I was there. Thoughts of those deep brown eyes and striking dimples battled with my professional interest until he looked back at the road.

Feeling embarrassed, I cleared my throat and fired off a question. "What, exactly, is the problem?"

"Pollution." The word shot back at me and I hastily wrote it down. My gloves made it difficult to hold the pen and I wished it weren't so cold.

"Pollution has been a problem for years.

Could you be a bit more specific?"

"Certainly. Oakwood's biggest industry is dumping toxic material into Lake Spencer."

Oakwood sits on the shore of Lake Spencer. We drink its water. We swim in it during the summer, skate on it in winter. Polluting it would definitely be a major problem.

"But Oakwood's biggest industry . . ." I began, shaking my pen at him.

"I know," he said, "only too well. Oakwood's biggest industry is Whitson, Incorporated. Do you mind if we stop for lunch?"

Chapter Two

Ross handed the menus back to the waitress after she'd taken our order. We had stopped at a cozy little Italian place about ten miles from Oakwood. I'd been here before and, apparently, so had he. We were sitting opposite each other in a tall-backed booth off in a corner. A pink carnation in a bud vase stood between us and Ross kept pushing the vase around nervously, fidgeting. My notebook was open and at the ready.

"The paper mill — Whitson, Incorporated — is owned by your family, right?" I asked, making a note on the paper.

"Yes, that's right. The mill is jointly owned by my sister, Marcia, and my Uncle Joseph. Marcia is president and has been for quite some time. She's technically Uncle Joe's boss, but that's on paper only. He actually sees to the day-to-day operation of the plant. They call him chief executive officer, a lofty title that agrees with him," Ross said with a hint of smile.

14

For as long as I could remember, the mill had been run by the short, white-haired man. We saw him regularly at the newspaper. Whitson, Incorporated, supplied our newsprint and he frequently stopped in to deliver advertisements for one of the company's products. Although he must be nearing sixty, he had looked the same for years. Gruff, no-nonsense, all business. That was Joseph Whitson.

"Does your uncle know about the pollution you claim is taking place?"

"I don't claim it, Lauren. I know it!" Ross stated emphatically. His hands were clenched into fists on the tabletop. His conviction blazed across at me.

I shifted in my seat, pulling one leg up under me and giving Ross a chance to calm down. "What does your sister say about all this? Surely you've gone to her with your suspicions."

He cleared his throat and looked away from me, reluctant to speak. "Well, that's another problem. Marcia is very fond of our uncle. When I tried to bring this subject up with her, she got very defensive. She thought I was making an unjustified attack." He shrugged.

"Even when you showed her evidence?"

He cut me off. "Marcia is difficult to understand or explain. What matters here is that the

15

lake is being polluted by Whitson, Incorporated!"

I asked the most important question. "How do you know about this? Who told you?"

His eyes, looking even darker in the dim interior, caught mine and shot away. "I can't tell you that. But I can tell you it's a very reliable source."

"An employee?" I guessed.

"Think what you want," Ross said, and I knew I was right.

If any of this checked out, it could be quite a story, I thought. A member of the family spilling the beans about environmental crime. Wheels started turning in my brain and I tapped my pen rhythmically against the edge of the table.

The waitress arrived just then with our salads and I waited to speak until after she had left.

"Your source — did he detail what Whitson is doing?"

"Oh, yes. He has documentation to prove that Federal pollution control standards aren't being met. The statistics submitted to the authorities are being falsified."

I consumed a forkful of lettuce, lightly seasoned and crisp. "That explains why the citizens of Oakwood haven't heard about this sooner," I said, putting down my fork and jotting Ross's comment into my notebook.

"Yes." Ross's voice grew animated as he went on. "Lauren, this pollution isn't just unsightly or bothersome. It's toxic! All sorts of chemicals and carcinogens are being dumped into Lake Spencer!"

I reached for my water glass to take a sip, but now thought better of it. What kind of contaminants filled our lake? I gave a shudder.

"It's frightening, all right," Ross agreed. His brow furrowed in concern. "It has to stop. The public must know."

Nodding, I speared a tomato wedge. We ate in silence, lost in our own dark thoughts. I felt honored that Ross had come to me with this story, but I still didn't understand why. As an alderman, he could just call a press conference and tell the world — well, our corner of it — all about Whitson.

The waitress set steaming plates of the restaurant's famous spaghetti in front of us and placed a basket filled with garlic bread at my elbow.

"Mm!" Ross leaned over his plate, inhaling the fragrant aroma. "This smells delicious," he said, picking up fork and spoon.

I watched as he deftly twirled noodles onto the fork into a perfect, bite-size bundle. My own attempts at the same action always resulted in trailing noodles and splashing sauce. Choosing the safe way out, I used my fork to cut the pasta.

"Scaredy-cat!" Ross teased and I had to laugh.

"You bet!" I said. "I've tried that before."

"But it's so easy. And a lot more fun. Here, watch." Slowly, he illustrated his noodle-winding technique, narrating as he went along. He popped the result into his mouth and chewed.

"So European," I drawled and he nodded his head. "Did you pick that up in Italy?"

"No, no. Learned it at my father's knee. You try it now."

He was certainly persistent about it, I thought, carefully turning my fork against the spoon. Only one overlong noodle dangled when I finished, but I managed to move it from the fork to my mouth without getting telltale tomato sauce on my sweater.

Ross clapped his hands in amusement and I felt my cheeks grow hot with embarrassment. "Thank you," I said, "but applause really isn't necessary. Tell me more about the mill."

Ross's smile faded away. "All business, huh? That must be why you're such a good reporter." He sounded a little disappointed.

I looked across at him, filled with an urge to correct his misconception. "I'm not a workaholic, not by any means. But I am supposed to be working now."

"True enough." He paused, handing me a slice of bread. When I reached for it, he held on. "I'd like to see you when you're not working, I think." His tone was light and conversational, but his expression was serious. I blinked first and gave the bread a gentle tug.

"Well, when you're sure, let me know," I said, trying for a jesting tone. It had been a long time since there'd been a man in my life. There had never been anyone serious or lasting. In the four years since college, my life had been taken up with my career, and that was just fine with me. I hadn't felt lonely — at least, not very often. Still, I couldn't deny a certain attraction to Ross.

Our fingers touched around the bread and it felt as if all my nerve endings were tingling. His hand dropped away and I set the bread on my plate, carefully brushing the crumbs from my fingers.

Just then, I heard a familiar sound. The steady beep-beep of an office pager intruded on our meal and Ross reached hurriedly into his pocket.

"Sorry," he said a bit sheepishly, putting the device on the table. "They won't let me leave the office without it." He chuckled and checked the phone number printed on the beeper's display. "Would you excuse me for a minute? This might be something important." Ross stood as he spoke, one hand moving automatically to straighten his tie.

I watched as he crossed the restaurant with the smooth, casual movements of an athlete. He was definitely a man who kept in shape, and I wondered for an instant what sport he played. As I brought my gaze back to our table, I realized I hadn't been the only person observing Ross's actions.

A few yards away, with a clear view of our table, a man sat alone. He had turned in his chair to see where Ross had gone, and now, as I watched, he turned back to face me. Was it my imagination or did he pause when he noticed my scrutiny?

Certainly, he looked away, down onto the table and his lunch, which cooled before him. All I could see was the shiny top of his head, where a few stray blond hairs were attempting to camouflage a bald spot. He was dressed like a businessman in a suit and tie, and maybe he actually was, but something seemed wrong. His furtive study of Ross, the way he avoided looking at me, even the way he'd chosen a table where we could be observed easily, made me think suddenly suspicious thoughts. I toyed with my pasta and came up with a plan.

By the time Ross returned five minutes later, I was ready.

"Well," I kidded, "did the city go bankrupt in your absence?"

"What?" Ross asked, as if his mind were elsewhere. I repeated my remark, although it didn't seem so funny the second time, and he replied, "No, no." He signaled for the waitress and our check. "Nothing so serious, I'm glad to report. Just a . . . constituent."

We finished our coffee and Ross caught my hand when I moved to gather my notes. "Lauren," he said, "I need to know that you'll pursue this story for me. Please say you will."

I'll admit I was intrigued by his claims of wrongdoing at the Whitson mill, and I probably would have gone ahead anyway, but the sight of that other man, dining alone and seeming so curious, made my decision easy. I gave his hand a squeeze.

"Yes, I'll check this out. But I'll need more information from you. I may even have to talk to your source."

He had been nodding in encouragement, but now he stopped and frowned. "Well, I don't know —" he began, and I cut him off.

"These are serious allegations that your friend is making. If you expect me to put my reputation on the line, I'll expect your full

21

cooperation in return." I delivered the lines sternly, brooking no argument.

Ross sighed. "I'll try," he said. It was the best that I could hope for.

"Good. We have a deal."

I slid my purse strap onto my shoulder after stowing my notebook within and together we walked to the coatroom. While Ross retrieved our garments, I turned and looked back into the dining room. As I'd expected, the man at the other table was observing us once more. For the first time, I got a clear look at his face and tried to commit it to memory, although there was nothing very distinctive about him. He had pudgy cheeks that made his eyes look even smaller and he was obviously nervous.

The coffee cup he held in one hand wobbled as our eyes met, and he moved rapidly to replace it on the saucer. A little too rapidly. Off balance, the cup fell over, sending the liquid over the table and onto his lap. His chair screeched on the floor as he shoved backward with a yelp. All heads turned his way.

I slid into my coat as the waitress hurried over to his table, rag in hand.

"No problem," I heard her say. "We'll clean it right up, sir. Accidents will happen."

"Let's go!" I hissed in Ross's direction,

putting my arm through his and giving a yank. "Now!"

He gave me a puzzled look, a question in his eyes. I inclined my head toward the door. He put his hand over my arm and we walked quickly from the building.

Blinking furiously at the glare of the snow in the fading sun, I followed him to his car. Our feet crunched rapidly over the newly fallen snow, still white and relatively untrodden in the parking lot. As Ross moved around the car to open the door for me, I waved him away.

"Just get in and drive, Ross. Hurry!" I felt a little awkward, acting on a hunch and seeming so mysterious about it, but Ross listened to my tone as well as my words and we both quickly hopped in and fastened our seat belts.

The engine started at once and Ross put it in gear. "Where should I drive, Lauren?" he asked.

I pointed. "Around the corner of the restaurant and out of sight. Wait for me there."

It took all of ten seconds to reach our location, and before the car had even stopped rolling, I had the door open. My heavy clothes underneath my winter coat made it difficult for me to move swiftly, but I closed the car door and crept rapidly along the wall of the building. At the corner, with Ross's car out of sight, I peered past the shrubbery that decorated the front of the restaurant.

Half hoping, half dreading, I held my breath and watched the main entrance. Just a few seconds passed before the heavy wooden door swung open and the balding blond man dashed out into the cold.

He stopped on the porch, his eyes scanning the parking lot. Even though I knew he couldn't possibly see me, I shrank closer to the wall. Brushing ineffectively at his damp, coffee-stained trousers, he turned and looked at the highway in both directions, muttering what I imagined were curses under his breath.

When it became apparent we were nowhere in sight, he buttoned up his topcoat and fished in his pocket for keys. He crossed the lot, getting into a dark blue car with rounded lines. In a moment, he pulled onto the road and headed north toward Oakwood.

I straightened from my bent-over position and pulled my collar tight around my neck. The temperature seemed to be dipping with the sun, which now rode low in the west. Breaking into a jog, I ran back to the car and climbed in beside Ross.

His hands gripped the steering wheel, opening and closing around it nervously. "Would you mind telling me what that was all about?" he demanded.

I brushed my hair back from my eyes and said simply, "You are being followed, Ross."

Chapter Three

I sat at my desk in the nearly empty office, chewing on the end of a pencil and thinking. Ross had dropped me off half an hour earlier, after listening patiently to my theory about the man in the restaurant.

"But why would he follow me?" he had asked as we drove into town.

"Well," I guessed, "it probably has something to do with what you told me about Whitson, Incorporated. Did you mention that information to anyone else?"

He'd thought for a good long while, his lips pressed together in concentration, then shook his head. "No," he said positively. "I didn't say a word to anyone but you."

We hadn't been able to come up with any explanations before arriving at the office. When I left him, it was with the promise to call the next day.

The notes on my page had grown as I brainstormed about what action I should take next. It was almost quitting time now, but first thing the next morning I'd delve into the newspaper files again so I could read up on the paper mill, which was the biggest employer in Oakwood. No words of a scandal connected to it had ever reached me before. Except for the occasional contract negotiations, the people who worked there seemed content enough. Wages were high, business was booming, jobs were secure — or at least as secure as possible in these uncertain times.

The second thing I'd do tomorrow was make an appointment to see someone out at Whitson. I'd tell them I was planning a story on the history of the company. There must be some kind of industrial anniversary coming up, I figured. Fifty years of paper production? Largest mill in the state? Surely I could produce a feasible reason to ask a few questions.

My heart gave a leap as I made my plans and I could almost feel the jolt of adrenaline that filled me with eager anticipation. My pencil took up a staccato rhythm on the desk blotter. Yes, this was why I'd taken up journalism. Here in Oakwood, investigative research was the exception rather than the rule, but even the seemingly routine jobs covering local government meetings had their moments. There were always questions to be asked — tough questions. Real questions some people would rather not answer. But I'd ask them anyway and give the citizens of Oakwood the facts they deserved.

I had the full approval of the newspaper's editor, Frank McLyle, even though he never came right out and said so. Frank is a veteran newspaperman, having worked on a big city daily for over thirty years before attempting to retire.

"I just couldn't stand all those empty hours, Laurie," he told me once. "Some folks like all that leisure time, but not me." He shook his head, thick salt-and-pepper hair still cut in the flattop of his youth. So he'd given up retirement and opted for the slower pace of the *Oakwood Herald* instead.

The paper had improved with his arrival. He ran a tight ship, not hesitating to criticize, although he was a bit too reluctant to praise. We admired him greatly, in spite of these traits, and tried even harder to measure up.

I picked up my notes and walked past the desks of the other reporters, too preoccupied to stop and chat with the only other person in the room. Turning left down the hall, I headed for Frank's office. It wasn't big or fancy by any means, decorated only with the awards he'd won over the years and his yellowing diplomas from college. The door was ajar as I approached. His name was painted on the smoked glass in big black letters. I tapped against it carefully and stuck my head into the room.

"Frank, do you have a minute?"

His feet were up on the bookcase behind his desk, his chair turned away from the door. Without looking at me, he said, "Sure, Laurie. Come on in." Slowly, he lifted his feet to the floor, then swiveled around to face me.

He looked tired. The lines in his face seemed deeper and the bags beneath his eyes more pronounced. He rubbed one hand vigorously across his face and gave a sigh. "What can I do for you?"

I sat down near the door and shifted uncomfortably. The heavy wood chair was straight-backed, which didn't encourage one to linger. "Is everything all right, Frank? You look beat."

He waved away my concern. "I'm just tired," he said. "You forget I'm an old man."

Frank usually had more energy at quitting time than I had fresh from eight hours sleep. This "old man" talk of his was a running gag and everyone knew it.

"Old, Frank? Not you!" I teased and he gave me a watery smile.

When he asked me again why I had come, I stopped wondering if he was really okay and told him my story. I left out the part about the man I thought was following Ross. It would be just like Frank to decide he'd better put some man on the story, in case it got dangerous.

After I'd finished, he sat quietly for a long time. His hands made a little steeple and he pressed his index fingers against his lips in his official thoughtful pose. "Hmm," he said at last. "Could be something, could be nothing. What's your gut tell you?" Frank is big on gut reactions.

"It tells me this is something," I said, leaning over to prop an elbow on his desk. "Whitson — Ross — is really concerned about this. I can't believe he'd get this upset over circumstantial evidence."

"Could it be spite?" he suggested. "Does he have it in for this uncle of his? The one who runs the mill." His brow wrinkled into a hundred fine lines and several deep creases. "Could it be bad blood?"

I sat back, the chair creaking in protest. I had no idea. "It could be," I admitted, but I didn't believe it for a minute. "Although that isn't the impression I got at all."

Frank spread his hands in an abbreviated shrug. "I'd say check a little behind the scenes. What's the setup with the family, that sort of thing. And at the same time, see what you can turn up about the mill. Discreetly, of course."

30

"Of course," I repeated, nodding. "So, I can go ahead with this?" I clarified, and he moved his head up and down in a slow, solemn motion.

"You have my permission." He held up a finger. "But if it checks out, there could be repercussions, you know. Are you prepared for that?"

I stood up, smiling. "Am I ready for a fight, you mean? You bet I am!"

He gave a bark of laughter. "Well, be careful. And keep me posted, will you?"

"Every day," I promised from the doorway. "Good night, Frank. And thanks."

Later that evening, after I'd made a simple dinner for myself and fed my cat, Hamlet, his usual fishy meal, I settled onto the sofa. I couldn't quite get the Whitson idea out of my head, and I wished I had stayed late at work to go through the historical files on both the family and the corporation.

Here at home, I felt powerless, stymied. It seemed as if I were wasting valuable time. My curiosity demanded satisfaction.

Hamlet leaped up next to me and curled against my thigh. My hand went out automatically to stroke his long, thick fur, getting lost in the tabby stripes of his coat. As I ran my hand over him again and again in an almost hypnotic fashion, my mind wandered.

In the funny way of the human brain, this momentary break produced a brilliant idea. If I couldn't rummage through the newspaper's records of Oakwood history, I'd just consult the next best source.

I left one hand on Hamlet while the other drew the telephone from the end table onto my lap. Punching in the numbers took just a few seconds, then the line began to ring.

"Hello?"

"Hi, Mom. It's Lauren. How are you?" The sound of her voice always brought a smile to my lips, and all the miles between Oakwood and Arizona disappeared in a flash. She and Dad had moved there just three years ago, for the sake of Dad's health, and there were times when I still missed them desperately. Mostly, I just missed them.

"Lauren, dear! It's good to hear your voice. We're fine. Are you?" Parental concern came over the wires and I could picture her frowning into the phone.

I hastened to reassure her. "I'm fine, Mom. I'm eating my vegetables and getting plenty of sleep."

"Don't tease, Lauren. Those things are important. But I have a feeling you didn't call just to chat."

"You're right. I was wondering if you

could tell me something about the Whitson family. It's for a story I'm working on this week."

Mom and Dad had lived in Oakwood for over forty years. Dad ran the hardware store and Mom was a beautician. She'd heard every rumor ever circulated and she had a memory like an elephant.

"What do you want to know?"

Hamlet rolled over, exposing the soft, downy fur of his belly to my fingers and emitting loud rumbling noises. I dutifully rubbed his tummy while I talked. "Well, first off, I'd like to know about Ross Whitson, the alderman."

"Have you met him?" Mom jumped in. "He's a very handsome young man." Her voice sounded hopeful and interested.

I sighed. "Yes, Mom, I've met him and he is very good-looking. But that's not what I wanted to discuss."

"Oh." The word was flat and I knew she was disappointed. She was always waiting for those wedding bells to ring for me. *Maybe someday they will,* I thought.

"I want some history on him. You know, the gossipy stuff newspapers don't print."

"Hmmm. Let me think. . . ."

Hamlet gave my hand a lick, then playfully sank his teeth into the fleshy part below my thumb. Cuddle time was at its usual abrupt end. He jumped down from the sofa and stalked off.

"Well, it's a long story, now that I think of it," Mom said. "Sad too. Do you have your notebook?"

After I retrieved it from my purse and turned to an empty page, she went on.

"Ross's father, Charles Whitson, inherited the mill from Ross's grandfather. I think his name was Henry, but don't quote me." She gave a laugh at her own joke. "Anyway, Charles was pretty much of a freethinker. He had all sorts of plans to improve the mill — expand, diversify. He always wanted to institute better conditions for the employees too. Quite a champion of the common man, you know."

I scribbled rapidly. "Go on."

"He'd only been at the helm about five years when there was an accident. The whole family — Charles and his wife, Mary, Ross and his sister, Marcia — were off on vacation. I think they'd been at some national park, camping and communing with nature. They'd taken a tiny little private plane and something went wrong. The plane crashed, killing Ross's parents and leaving his sister in critical condition. Ross had a couple of broken bones, but that was all. He was lucky.

They never found out just what happened."

My pen halted and hovered over the page. Lucky? His parents suddenly killed, and his sister seriously injured? "What a horrible thing!" I said as a chill chased its way up my spine. "How awful!"

We were both quiet for a moment as I digested this news. Then I asked, "How old was Ross when it happened? Why don't I remember hearing any of this?"

"Well, this happened long, long ago. Ross was just a boy. Eight years old? Maybe nine? You were still in diapers then."

"Oh." I doodled a little in the margin of my paper. "What happened then? Who took care of them? Did Marcia recover without complications?"

She answered my last question first. "Unfortunately, no. She lives not too far from Oakwood. She's confined to a wheelchair, but is lively and intelligent and as active as possible. In fact, she works with her uncle at the mill. She's the president, you know." I could tell this impressed Mom by the way she emphasized the title. "She was tiny when the accident occurred, only six, if I recall. She probably doesn't even remember a time when she wasn't handicapped."

I thought of Ross at lunch that day, smiling and twirling spaghetti. *At my father's knee,* he had said, with no indication at all of the tragedy in his past.

"After their parents died," Mom started up again, "the kids were taken in by their uncle, Joseph Whitson. He also was given control of the mill, acting as a sort of regent until the children reached adulthood."

I frowned, using the end of my pencil to scratch my temple. "Ross and Marcia were supposed to run the mill?"

"Yes, that was the plan, according to Charles's will. But, as it turned out, of course, Ross had other ideas."

Somehow, that statement did not surprise me. He seemed like a man who knew his own mind.

"What were his plans?"

"You have to remember he came from a background that was both wealthy and altruistic. When he turned eighteen, he did something we all said he'd regret someday." She paused for dramatic effect, waiting for me to prod her along.

"What, Mom? What did he do?" I was sitting up straighter now, eager to hear.

Mom took a deep breath. "He signed over his share of the mill to his sister and his uncle. Said he wanted no part of it whatsoever."

Well, this was news!

"He gave Marcia the bulk of his shares in

the business. It almost seemed at the time as if he gave his uncle a percentage as an afterthought. Or an incentive to leave him alone, maybe," she brainstormed. "Sort of like a dog begging for table scraps," she went on. "You remember Taffy, the spaniel we had when you were little?"

"Yes, Mom." I wondered where this was leading.

"Well, she used to beg for food and I knew it was bad for her, but she was so persistent and she looked so sad that eventually I always gave in."

"Are you saying Ross gave in to his uncle and threw him stocks in the mill like table scraps?" I asked.

"Laugh if you will, dear, but that was the scuttlebutt at the time." Mom's voice dropped low. "Just between us, dear, I've never really liked Joseph Whitson. Oh, he comes off charming when he wants to, which isn't very often. But, mostly, he seems sneaky. I think he was quite pleased to get such a piece of the mill. He paid Ross some token sum for his interest in the company. But, if I know him, it was far below the real value. Yet Ross accepted it."

"Hmm. Why didn't Ross want the mill? What drove him away?" I asked.

"He was eighteen, just out of school. You

know how idealistic people can be at that age. Ross was no exception. He wanted to save the world singlehandedly. He joined the Peace Corps and went overseas. Quite admirable, really," she concluded.

"I should say so!" I exclaimed, glad to hear Ross had such a compassionate nature. I wondered why that discovery pleased me.

"Yes. He got some sort of allowance from his parents' estate. Marcia did too. After his stint abroad, he went to college, then to law school. One of those big-name ones. I forget which. Something back East."

"And came back to Oakwood as a full-fledged attorney?" I guessed.

"Exactly."

I made a few more notes on a fresh page. "Uncle Joseph's been working at the mill for an awfully long time. I wonder if Ross has ever been sorry he gave it all away."

"I can't answer that, Lauren. Why don't you just give him a call and ask?" Mom suggested. I knew she was teasing me, ready to get back on the subject of my marital status.

I took a deep breath. "Now, Mom. . . ."

Chapter Four

True to my word, the next morning I was parked at the microfilm reader at the newspaper, flipping back through the years one page at a time. My topic today was Whitson the company, and there was plenty to read. Everything from their annual donation to the public library to their year-end report was duly noted by the *Herald*. We're a "local news" kind of paper, rather than an "issues of the day" type, so references to things like pollution were limited to articles on car emissions and recycling.

For over an hour, my eyes scanned the screen for any hint of helpful information. I made notes of dates when articles relating to the mill were published, in case I needed to look them up again. Around ten-thirty, I trudged back to my desk with my third cup of coffee and put in a call to Whitson's main office.

The secretary put me through to the public-relations department, which suited my purposes just right. I told the man I talked to, a Mr. North, an interesting story about an article I was supposedly working on.

"It's about Oakwood's economy in these hard times," I said, "spotlighting the companies that help to keep us afloat." It couldn't hurt to butter them up a little, I figured.

Before I knew it, I was being invited to come down to the main office, where I could feel free to use all the historical information they had and ask whatever questions I wanted.

"We'd be pleased to help you with your article, Miss Sterling. We're proud of the contributions we make to Oakwood. It's a wonderful town and we're happy to call it our home," Mr. North said.

I grimaced at this sugary speech and drew little smiling faces along the edge of my desk blotter as he went on — and on. Eventually, he wound down and we confirmed our appointment for the next day. I hung up the phone with a sense of relief, penciling the scheduled time onto my calendar.

Of course, this Whitson story wasn't my only topic for next week's paper. I spent the remainder of the day working on other things, and before I knew it, the clock said five.

I turned up my coat collar against the cold wind that was blowing and trudged out to my car. It complained a bit, but eventually the engine turned over and I headed for home.

The weather forecasters were promising something resembling spring for Friday, so I dressed that morning in a compromise outfit — a pastel pink dress of soft jersey. The color was like spring; the long sleeves and turtleneck like winter. Ivory pumps and pale nylons completed the look and I added just a simple strand of pearls.

Sure enough, the breeze that greeted me as I left the house did hold a whisper of spring. On my way to the car. I took a moment to lift my face to the sun and breathe deeply, taking in the fresh, clean smell of the air. If the weather held, a walk in the woods would definitely be in order for the weekend. With that cheery thought, I hoisted the heavy garage door.

Oakwood is a small town, and the Whitson mill is located right at the eastern edge of it, smack on the shore of Lake Spencer. As I turned into the gate of the plant, I could see the glistening water just beyond. Sunlight danced off it in ever-changing patterns that made a dazzling display. Watching it, my heart grew heavy. If Ross Whitson were correct, even now the water was being polluted, toxic substances being dumped into its once-pristine water to fester and destroy.

I pulled to a stop while I pondered the lake. Then I shoved the car into gear with a forceful hand and drove on. If this crime was really happening, I'd let the whole world know about it. This could be the most important story of my career. Not just for me, but for all of Oakwood. I gritted my teeth and parked in a spot near the door labeled VISITORS. Determination set my shoulders as I marched up the front steps of the old, brick building.

It didn't take long to get directions to the public-relations department. My heels clicked rhythmically as I advanced down the corridor, which resembled an aged high school — high ceilings with plenty of doors on either side of the hall. My head swiveled from one side to the other looking for the one marked PUBLIC RELATIONS. Eventually, I found it.

The door opened with a squeak and a woman at a desk just inside looked up. She gave me a smile, looking from the clock on the wall to the appointment book in front of her.

"Good morning. Miss Sterling?"

I nodded. "Yes, I have an appointment with Mr. North."

Mr. North was duly summoned and appeared in a matter of minutes. He was several inches shorter than my five feet ten inches and had gone a bit paunchy with middle age. The hand he extended was pudgy and hot. I quickly released it, returning his smile with one of my own. After I'd made a few introductory remarks about my article, he jumped in, waving me into another room that apparently served as the company's archives.

"Here is the history of Whitson, Incorporated," he said with a flamboyant gesture. I looked around the room, which was filled with file cabinets and bookcases.

Pictures of Whitson then and now lined the walls. A huge hand-tinted portrait of the company's founder, Ross's great-grandfather, took pride of place between the windows. I made the appropriate oohs and aahs and Mr. North turned pink with pleasure. Here was a man who loved his job.

"Well, I'll leave you to your research, then," he said as I seated myself at the long table that ran down the center of the room. "If you need me, I'll be just around the corner."

"Right." I smiled. "Thank you."

Once alone, I worked diligently, skimming rapidly through the files dealing with the company's early years. As I'd suspected, most of what I found showed the mill in a favorable light. The folder dealing with the strike of 1973 was a bit more interesting, but still not what I was looking for. To keep up appearances, I took plenty of notes and made copies of several articles on the machine in the outer office.

On one of the bookcase shelves, I found a stack of industry publications. They seemed like a better place to look for critical articles than Whitson-produced pamphlets. I pushed up my sleeves and carried the stack to my workplace, scanning each issue's table of contents. Eagerly, I read through the half-dozen articles that dealt with pollution-control standards and the difficulties some mills were encountering from environmental protection groups. Had Whitson ever run into trouble? I wondered. I spent another ten minutes at the copy machine, then returned the magazines to their shelf. As I turned away from the bookcase, Mr. North tapped on the doorjamb.

"How's it going?" he asked. "Need any help?"

I shook my head. "No, thank you. The files have been very helpful." I waved my handful of copies as evidence. "Especially these magazines."

Mr. North's brow furrowed and cleared. "I thought the article was to be about our company specifically," he said.

I put the papers into my folder and snapped it shut. "Oh, it is, it is. But looking at these helped give me a better perspective — you know, a fuller understanding of the paper industry itself."

He nodded in a distracted way, as if he didn't quite follow my reasoning.

"Tell me," I went on, "several of these publications contain articles on older mills and how they have difficulty keeping up with technological advances and improvements." I shrugged nonchalantly. "Things like recycling paper, cutting toxic emissions, being energy-efficient."

Mr. North began to nod, increasing the speed of the movement as I ticked off the items. I hurried on to my question. "Has Whitson ever run into trouble like that?"

"Oh, no," he hastened to reassure me. "The physical plant here is old, that's true, but we have always maintained the highest industry standards. Mr. Whitson has continuously upgraded the operation to keep the mill competitive." He puffed out his chest, as if taking credit for the accomplishment. "We are proud to be top-of-the-line."

I nodded. "And well you should be," I said, gathering up my purse and following him to the door. "Thanks again for all your help. I'll be in touch if I need anything further." I quickly shook his sweaty hand once more, and started back down that long corridor to the parking lot.

Despite outward appearances, it hadn't been a wasted morning. On the drive back to the newspaper office, I worked on the opening sentence of my first article on the mill.

On Saturday morning, the sun was shining and a warm breeze blew from the southwest. I opened a window to let the fresh air in while I indulged in the mundane but necessary weekly cleaning. Hamlet promptly took up his spot on the windowsill, his quivering nose pressed to the screen.

I almost didn't hear the phone over the roar of the vacuum and hurried into the kitchen to answer it.

"Lauren!" Ross's voice, warm and lively, came over the line.

I smiled, glad to hear from him. "Hello, Ross. What's up?"

"The sun and the temperature," he quipped. "I wondered if you'd like to join me for a walk this afternoon?"

My eyes roamed quickly around the room. I've never been one to obsess about sparkling floors and appliances and, besides, the place didn't look too bad. The choice was easy to make. "Sure, I'd like that. Pick me up around one?" I gave him my address and simple directions. "I'm right on the corner. The brick Cape Cod with blue dormers."

"Gotcha. See you then."

When I hung up the phone, I was still smiling. I finished my cursory brand of house-work while humming a tune. Hamlet meowed in protest. He'd never liked my singing.

When Ross arrived, I was sitting on the front porch, waiting for him. I wore a heavy red sweatshirt with a T-shirt underneath and a pair of worn, but still acceptable, jeans. Instead of sneakers, I'd chosen low rubber-ized boots, which are better for muddy ter-rain.

Ross's silver car was even shinier than the last time I'd seen it, so I figured he had just made a trip to the car wash. He honked the horn as he pulled in the drive and I waved as I got to my feet.

Really! I thought, forcing myself to stand still as he approached. There was no need for my heart to be thumping this way. No reason for the slight shaking in my knees. We were working on a story together and this walk was just, well, a relaxing recess from all the serious stuff. Still, I greeted him with a big smile and noticed with pleasure that he returned it watt for watt.

I'm fortunate enough to live just one block from the park that runs along the lakeshore. The paper mill is about three miles north, pretty much out of sight from my location, making the park a scenic delight of trees and sky. We headed off in that direction, making small talk about the weather, and, within ten minutes, were deep in the woods.

We wandered slowly along the well-trodden path, stepping carefully around the puddles left by the melting snow. The trees overhead seemed to be filled with birds calling out songs I hadn't heard since the autumn, so very long ago.

Ross came to a stop, tipping back his head and taking a deep breath. "Ah!" he sighed. "Spring has sprung. Isn't it wonderful?"

He looked at me, his eyes shining with genuine pleasure. As I bobbed my head in agreement, he took his hands from the pockets in his denim jacket and reached for mine. Giving them a squeeze, he said, "On days like this, it's hard to believe there are problems in the world. And in our town. Hard to believe this air isn't as clean as it should be. That the lake isn't the crystal-clear wonder it seems from here."

My hands fit easily into his, nestled warm and snug. For a moment, I concentrated on that feeling more than on his words. Eventually, they penetrated and I said, "Maybe that's why we get days like this. To lift our spirits and inspire us."

Tilting his head to one side, he pondered my idea. "That's pretty profound, Lauren. I think you might be on to something."

I laughed. "I minored in philosophy at college, you know. Old habits die hard." I gave a tug on his hand. "Follow me."

These were my woods. I walked them often, and had for years. Leading the way along the foot-wide path bordering the bluff, I set a steady pace. We were climbing and it was a bit perilous. The ground was slippery with mud and I was glad I'd worn my boots.

Behind me, Ross began to grumble. "Hey, Lauren, slow down. We could get hurt here. It's a long way down." He sounded anxious.

I glanced back over my shoulder. The wind caught at my hair and I pushed it away with a laugh. "It's okay, Ross. I've walked this trail a million times. The tree roots are just like steps up ahead here."

Sure enough, my toe stubbed on a jutting root as I spoke. I fell forward, my hands landing heavily on the squishy earth. In the second it took me to tumble, I felt a flash of fear. As Ross had pointed out, we were up high, with the edge of the cliff just a few feet away. But I clung tightly to the root and pushed myself back up. Ross reached out to steady me as I rose, helping me to regain my footing.

"Are you all right? Boy, you gave me a start!" His eyebrows met when he frowned, I noticed. He led me off the path into the tall, brown grass. The mud sucked at my boots as we walked, our progress slow. When we were what Ross deemed a safe distance from the cliff, he turned to face me.

"You could have gone over the edge back there, and broken a bone — or worse!" He gave my shoulders a gentle shake and my hands went up against his chest, resting on the heavy denim of his jacket. "Don't do that again!"

"You might not be here to save me next time, huh?" I teased. It seemed he was over-reacting to my spill. There was mud on my knees, but I was unharmed. I wasn't about to pull away, though, from this cozy, windswept embrace.

"And that could be tragic," he echoed my tone, jesting now that I was safe. The faintest grin curved his lips upward. He tugged me a little closer, the flicker of smile sliding away.

For the space of a heartbeat, our faces hovered near one another. Then, as my eyes closed, I felt his lips touch mine. Soft and tender, his kiss stirred me, causing a flutter in my stomach and a whirling in my brain. I could only guess at Ross's reaction to the kiss. By the time my eyes had opened once more, his smile was back in place.

"You look pretty with your hair all mussed," he told me and I laughed.

"Thank you," I said.

He slipped his arm around my shoulders and we trudged off into the woods once more, our silence companionable and contented.

Eventually, we came upon the clearing that served as a picnic area in summer. The tables weren't out yet, so we had to content ourselves with perching on the top rung of the split-rail fence bordering the bluff. Below us, nearly one hundred feet down at this point, the waves of Lake Spencer lapped at the shore. Each year, erosion takes a bigger toll on the land, eating away at the dirt and sand. The wind, which only helps speed the destructive process, felt wild and powerful as it whipped my hair into my eyes. I tossed my head to send it flying and turned to Ross.

He had a marvelous profile. The stern jawline and straight nose made him look like a sea captain as he surveyed the lakefront. I took this quiet moment to think about him. I wondered at the turmoil he must feel inside. His father had worked hard to make the world — especially Oakwood — a better place. Now, his family's company might be responsible for a major environmental threat. How tormenting to think of the ironies there, to somehow feel responsible for it all.

"A penny for your thoughts," I said at last.

He shook his head, giving a snort of sarcastic laughter. "Don't think they're worth that much right now." His voice was low and thick.

Reaching over, I placed my hand on his. "It'll work out," I reassured him. He turned to me with a question in his eyes. "This mill thing," I explained. "It will all come out. You'll see."

He nodded very slowly and gave my fingers a squeeze. "That's what I'm afraid of," he said.

I puzzled over that remark, but didn't press him. Instead, I told him about my trip to Whitson the day before. He chuckled over my description of Mr. North.

"He's quite a cheerleader for the company," he said. "Just what a public-relations person should be, I guess."

"I guess," I agreed reluctantly.

"Did you turn up anything useful?"

I shrugged my shoulders and mentioned the industry magazines and the articles I'd made copies of. "I'll show them to you when we get back," I said. "I think I've got the angle I want for this story."

We climbed down from the fence and headed back to the house, our conversation drifting onto other topics. In no time, my little house could be seen and, as always, it gave me a warm feeling inside.

As we walked on, I told Ross about how I'd lived there my whole life; how, when Mom and Dad moved to Arizona, I'd bought it for myself.

"I couldn't stand the thought of someone else living in it," I said with a grin.

We came to a stop on the sidewalk out in front, inspecting the house as it sat in the sunshine. A flagstone walk curved up to the front porch, where a white wooden swing big enough for two swayed in the breeze. The window boxes here in front got the light almost all day and already the first green hint of my spring blossoms pushed through the soil. In a month, the boxes would burst with color.

"It's charming," Ross said, taking in the cozy picture it made. "It's like you."

I shot a glance at him from the corner of my eye and didn't fight the smile that crept across my face. "Do you have time to stop in?" I asked, trying not to sound eager.

"I've got all afternoon," he said, following me up the walk.

Inside, I directed him to the sofa and made the necessary introductions. "This is Hamlet," I said, picking up the ten-pound cat and giving him a hug. "Hamlet, this is Ross."

Ross held out a hand and let Hamlet sniff it. "Pleased to meet you," he said, scratching behind one furry ear when Hamlet obligingly tilted his head. To me, he said, "Why is he called Hamlet? Are you a fan of the Bard?"

"Well, of course, but I didn't name him." I set the cat down and he walked in circles around our ankles, rubbing up against us and purring. "Dad did. He thought it was fitting for a Norwegian forest cat. That's Hamlet's breed," I explained.

Ross frowned and said politely, "But Hamlet was from Denmark."

I laughed. "Tell that to Dad, will you? I've already tried."

Leaving the two of them to get better acquainted, I went to the kitchen for refreshments. When I reentered the living room, Hamlet was sprawled on his back and Ross was rubbing his tummy, talking in a low tone.

I set down the tray I carried. "You seem to be getting along."

Ross straightened, grinning sheepishly. "Yes. Animals like me."

"Because you like them," I said. "They can tell." I handed him a glass of orange juice and sipped my own. "Let's talk about the mill."

"Okay. Show me the articles you found."

He read them over rapidly. The pages

already were covered with yellow highlighter and questions I'd scrawled in the margins. When he finished, he said, "Now, tell me your angle, as you put it. What will your article say?"

I shifted on the cushions and thought out loud. "I see this as several articles, actually, since I don't have very much to put in the first one. I'm planning to give a history of the mill, comparing its past role in Oakwood to its role today. You know, economic impact, number of local employees, things like that. Then I thought I'd do a paragraph near the end on the environment. How, fifty years ago, no one really looked too far down the road as far as toxins were concerned. As with landfills, we just figured there would always be a place to dump stuff. I'm going to end it by mentioning the current laws on pollution and the difficulties some mills across the country have run into in trying to obey them. Then, next week, the whole focus of my story will be on Whitson, and its efforts to comply."

Ross tapped an index finger against his cheek. "Will they give you that information?" he asked. "Willingly?"

I picked up a Whitson brochure from the stack of papers beside me. "Some of it is detailed right here."

Ross took the glossy pamphlet from my

hand and flipped through it briefly. It was filled with color photographs of both the mill and our town. Anyone seeing it without visiting Oakwood would think we were the original Small Town, U.S.A. There were shots of little children eating ice-cream cones, the town Christmas tree lit up at night, flags flying, and autumn leaves falling. In between the pictures, the story of the paper mill was told.

"There's a section on the environment and Whitson's vow to protect it," I said, pointing.

"Yes, here it is. *Into the future*. Very catchy."

When I glanced up to see if he was serious, he wrinkled his nose. "But how will this expose what I've told you?"

I smiled. "I believe in hunches, and something tells me an article on Whitson that even hints at the pollution laws will produce a definite reaction before next week."

"Hm. Sounds devious. And clever." He snapped the brochure shut and gave it a well-aimed toss onto the coffee table. "I like it."

Chapter Five

Frank liked it too. It was hard to tell, actually, because Frank isn't very demonstrative. When he read the article and heard my plan, however, he gave a barely perceptible nod. I knew I'd aced it when he said, "This reminds me of the old days on the *Gazette*." He tapped the papers against his leg and got a far-off look in his eye. "We had some exciting times then. Chasing crooks, tracking down clues, working for justice."

I laughed. "You sound like Batman," I said, picturing my editor in cape and cowl.

A hint of a smile passed over his face and when he looked at me, his eyes were twinkling. "It's noble work we do, Lauren. Never forget that." Holding up one index finger, he boomed out one of his favorite expressions: "Truth above all."

I nodded. "Right, Frank. That's what I'm aiming for with this. The truth."

He handed the papers back to me. "I'm sure you'll get it."

Several days later, I recalled his words in wry amusement, wondering if he'd even had a hint about what else I would get.

The first call came in on Thursday afternoon. That week's edition wasn't even in the mailboxes of the people farther out in the countryside. It had been delivered to the local newsstands just hours before and already, action had begun.

"Miss Sterling, this is Dennis North of Whitson, Incorporated." His voice had the false note of enthusiasm I'd been aware of while at the mill.

I reached for my notebook. "Hello, Mr. North. What can I do for you?" A simple question. It did not receive a simple answer. The P.R. man earned his keep that day by using plenty of fancy phrases and big words, all sending the same message — leave the story alone.

"As I've stated, Whitson meets or exceeds Federal pollution control standards. We would be pleased to supply you with the figures to prove it, although I'm afraid Oakwood's readers might find it terribly tedious." He gave a cheerless chuckle.

I chose my words with care. "Well, thank you. I'd be pleased to see those statistics. And I think I can say with certainty that Oakwood's residents would find it interesting.

Everyone cares about the quality of the water they drink, Mr. North."

"Of course, Miss Sterling! Of course they do!" he blustered. "I didn't mean to imply. . . . That is, I. . . . Well, it's just so technical."

I sketched a smokestack onto the margin of my paper, adding great billows of smoke and a frown instead of a smile. "Leave that part to me. I'm sure I'll be able to interpret it all. Could you have the statistics to me by Monday?"

He assured me he could and I hung up.

A moment later the phone rang again. I caught it up, tucking it between my ear and shoulder.

"*Oakwood Herald.* Lauren Sterling speaking." For a minute, there was silence on the line and I wondered if it were a wrong number. Still, whoever was there didn't hang up, didn't even breathe. Suddenly, my attention was caught and I sat up straighter, straining my ears.

Unexplainably, a shiver crept up my spine and I knew in an instant that I didn't want to hear whatever this caller had to say. My hand tightened on the receiver and I moved it away from me, ready to hang up, when the raspy voice began.

"People who ask questions don't always like the answers they get."

It could have been a man's voice, or a woman's. The person spoke faintly and without emotion. But with plenty of menace.

"Who is this?" I demanded. "This is the *Oakwood Herald.*"

"Keep that pretty little nose out or it could get cut off!" The line went dead, the dial tone buzzing in my ear.

I sat frozen. All around me business as usual took place — typewriters clacked, phones rang, people talked. And yet, I was oblivious. The shiver I'd felt earlier moved from my spine to my limbs and I felt my knees quaking. It irritated me to see my hand shake as I returned the receiver to its cradle.

I'd been threatened.

A deep breath helped me to catch my thoughts as they spun in circles. I had no doubt the call had been in reference to the Whitson story. My other features in this week's paper had included a riveting account of the Common Council meeting, three paragraphs on the wrestling meet last weekend, and an interview with a local resident who had been a game-show contestant on national television. None of those stories invited sinister phone calls. No, it had to be the mill.

I pulled my pen from where I'd tucked it behind my ear and drummed it rhythmically on the desk top. I'd expected Mr. North's phone call. I had not expected the other.

Closing my eyes, I concentrated on the few words the caller had spoken, trying to hear the voice again in my head. It would be almost impossible to identify, I decided. It had been toneless and cold, delivering the lines by rote.

Swiftly, I wrote down the sentences in my notebook, although there was no doubt I'd ever forget them. The chill I'd felt had long since left me, replaced by confusion and a feisty spark of anger. So, someone wanted me off this story enough to make veiled, anonymous threats. That had to mean there was something to hide at Whitson. That could easily mean Ross's story was true.

Ross. Just the thought of him helped steady my nerves. I pictured him sitting in my living room, stroking Hamlet's belly with gentle fingers. He had won Hamlet's trust completely. He had a very good start on mine.

With a baleful glance at the telephone, I left my desk and crossed the room to the community coffee pot. It was nearly empty.

While my hands went through the mechanics of starting a fresh pot, my mind wandered off on its own. I remembered that Frank had told me to check on the family last week. I felt a twinge of conscience.

Mom was definitely a fountain of information, but she couldn't really know how family feelings ran. I hadn't even brought up the subject with Ross. It was a little bit ticklish, after all. I couldn't just say, "Do you have a grudge against your uncle, Ross? Are you making this up because of some personal vendetta?"

I poured water into the coffee maker, punched the button marked BREW, and leaned up against the counter to wait. As soon as I returned to my desk, I'd call Ross. If I was going to pursue this story, I needed more from him — more background, more personal history, more details.

The fresh-brewed smell of coffee filled the air and I couldn't wait any longer. In a tricky, awkward fashion, I filled my cup as the machine still ran, and took a sip as I carried my mug back to my desk.

Ross's secretary put me right through, and he greeted my call with enthusiasm.

"Saw the story, Lauren! It looks terrific. I like the way you hint at next week's article without coming right out and saying it."

"Thanks, I learned that from politicians like you," I joked. His laugh came across the line, hearty and sincere. He certainly didn't sound like a man trying to hide anything.

"I need to see you and ask you some questions," I stated in my most businesslike manner. "I need some details about the allegations you've made regarding the mill. Now I need some facts."

"Well, Lauren, I'll show you everything I've seen and bring you copies of the papers and all. Is that what you mean?"

"Yes, exactly." I thought of my phone call and wondered if now was the time to confide in Ross. Maybe it would be better to tell him in person. "I'm sure you'll be glad to hear I've already received quite a response to the article," I said, keeping my voice light. "Sooner than I'd expected."

"Hey, that's great! Just like you said, right? Lauren, that's incredible."

More than you know, I thought. "Well, it's a step in the right direction, I hope," I said.

My guarded tone was evident, I'm sure, because he asked quickly, "Is anything wrong? Are you all right?"

I nodded. "I'm fine. I'll tell you all about it when I see you."

"I'll stop by tonight. There's a meeting of the transportation committee, but it shouldn't go long. I'll be by around eight."

"That'll be fine." It was two-thirty now. I'd have plenty of time to get at my other work and still stop in at the local library to do a bit of research.

"I'll leave the porch light on," I promised.

The next time the phone at my desk rang, I

gave a nervous start and let it go on jangling while I convinced myself to answer it. I nearly laughed out loud in relief when it turned out to be Andrew Brown, the fire chief. Cheerfully, I took down the details of the upcoming "Stamp out fires" smoke-detector program, then turned my attention to the projects before me. It wasn't easy to push the mill into the back of my mind, but once I did, it stayed there.

At nine-thirty that night, I sat alone on my sofa, papers scattered all around me. I'd tidied up the place, baked a batch of cookies, and reapplied my lipstick. Ross had said he'd be by after his meeting. About eight, he had said.

When the clock on the mantel chimed the half hour, I knew he wouldn't be coming. Setting down the pamphlet I held, I heaved a sigh. This was very disappointing, for several conflicting reasons. First, of course, I told myself, because I wanted answers to my questions. Second, I had to admit, I just wanted to see him.

I pressed my lips together and frowned. This was a business appointment. He could have called to cancel our plans. Is this the way he treated his clients too?

"Remind me never to see him about legal

trouble, Hamlet," I said to the cat, asleep on a chair across the room. "He'd probably never show up in court!" My words were sarcastic and angry. Hamlet opened one eye, yawned, and went back to sleep.

I busied myself clearing away the papers and the tray I'd set on the coffee table. I'd already eaten most of the cookies, and now seemed like as good a time as any to finish them off. I set the tray on the kitchen counter and took another peanut butter kiss from the plate.

I'd just taken a bite when the phone rang.

"Finally!" I said, chewing rapidly. I picked up the phone, swallowed, and said, "Hello?"

Ross's deep voice did not greet me. Just as my call at the office began in silence, so did this one.

"Hello!" I repeated sternly, trying to sound fierce and unafraid, although my heart had begun to pound and my hands were already shaking. Dragging the extra-long cord behind me, I crossed the kitchen to the back door, double-checking the dead bolt. I peered out into the quiet yard, but all was peaceful.

"We're watching you." The voice was the same, raspy and muffled.

I dropped the curtain back into place as if it had burned my fingers. "Who is this?" I demanded, stuttering a bit on the first word.

"Just a friend. A friend who doesn't want to see you get hurt. And you won't if you know when to stop."

"Is this about Whitson? Is this about the mill?" I didn't think I'd get an answer, and I was right. The caller hung up without another word.

Carefully, I returned the receiver to the cradle, concentrating on the motion to settle my nerves. There are times — most times — when I love my independence and enjoy being on my own. Sometimes, though, I wish I didn't live alone. Sometimes, it gets a little too quiet. Like now.

Before I climbed uneasily into bed that night, I made sure all the windows were locked and all the shades pulled down. I even took the ultimate safety precaution of putting a chair under the doorknob. With Hamlet curled up at my feet, I forced my eyes closed and attempted to sleep. After a few false starts, I succeeded, dreaming of running and falling and screaming. And running and falling and screaming.

I woke up with a headache.

Chapter Six

All the next day, I expected to hear from Ross or my mysterious "friend," but I was doomed to failure. The day passed slowly and entirely without incident. I worked a bit on next week's story about pollution laws, using the information I'd picked up at the library the day before. Mr. North had had a point when he said the information was complicated. I needed a lawyer to interpret some of the convoluted sentences, but the only lawyer I knew was Ross, and he was unavailable.

I'd tried calling his office early in the day, but his secretary said he wasn't in. She didn't know when he would be around, but promised to tell him I had called. This was of little comfort.

At noon, I took my tomato sandwich and chips into Frank's office and we had a chat over lunch. I hadn't planned to tell him about the calls. I knew he'd fret and give me a lecture. Still, the minute he said, "How's the Whitson piece coming, Laurie?", I threw caution to the wind and it all poured out. I did manage to keep quiet about the man I'd seen following Ross, although I privately wondered if he were the anonymous phone caller.

To my surprise, Frank brushed off the implied threats. "Oh, don't let it worry you too much," he said, reaching for my bag of potato chips. He crunched his way through half of them as he spoke. "You ruffled a few feathers and somebody's nervous. Maybe they've got a big government deal coming up — computer paper for Federal office buildings or something, and they don't want any bad publicity."

I thought about that. It could be true. "But wouldn't it be easier just to tell me that? Why try to scare me? Why threaten to break my nose?" I reached up and touched it. It had always been a bit too long for my taste, but I still considered it an essential part of my anatomy.

Frank laughed. "Laurie, Laurie. No one is going to break your nose. Believe me. When I worked in the city, threats of bodily harm were part and parcel."

I knew he meant to be reassuring. "Were any ever carried out?" I asked.

He made a big production out of crushing the chip bag and lobbing it into the garbage can across the room. "That's not the point, Laurie."

"Well, it is to me!"

"You want off the story?" he offered casually, knowing full well I'd refuse. "I can put Mitch on it if you want."

Mitch! Mitch, the sportswriter!

I stood up, placing my balled fists onto the desk top. "No, Frank. You know I won't give in. I'll follow this story wherever it goes." I thought of Ross, suddenly absent and unavailable. "Wherever it goes," I repeated.

After clearing it with Frank, I arranged to leave work an hour early. I could accomplish just as much at home. Maybe more.

As I pulled out of the parking lot, I noticed a dark-colored car sitting at the curb. It looked rather familiar, but I didn't place it until I glanced in the rearview mirror and saw it pulling away. I thought I caught a flash of blond hair, but I couldn't be certain. Could it be the same man who had followed Ross the day of our initial meeting?

At the first stoplight, I checked in the mirror again. There he was, not directly behind me, but with one car separating us. My hands clenched the wheel when I realized I was his target of surveillance today. I had never expected anything like this to happen, and tried to remember what television detectives did to "lose a tail." The thought of pushing my aging Mustang into a high-speed chase and squealing around corners was almost enough to make me laugh.

The car behind me gave an impatient blast of its horn as the light turned green. I stepped on the gas. Driving slowly, dividing my time between watching the road in front of me and the car behind, I turned a few corners and the dark car dutifully followed. It always remained far enough away so I couldn't see the driver clearly.

I was in the business section of town now, where miniature strip malls and fast-food restaurants had sprung up over the last few years. Just past Pizzaville was the car wash, and, impulsively, I pulled in. My car was dirty; it could use a bath and, perhaps, with luck, the man following me would give up and go away rather than wait for me in the parking lot. To the best of his knowledge, I reasoned, I didn't even know he was there. If he stayed in one place for the ten minutes the wash took, I might notice and become suspicious. Would he risk that?

I paid my money and followed the attendant's hand signals to the automated track. Only then did I look again in the mirror.

The blue car was pulling in behind me! Apparently, we would go through the wash together. The first spray of water hit the windows and obliterated the car from view. I spun and faced forward as various sponges and brushes whirled and slid over the car. It was noisy inside with the water splashing and engines running, but even that cacophony couldn't drown out my thoughts.

I caught my lower lip between my teeth and worried. I had to see Ross, and it had to be soon. But if I drove to his office now, the person following me would know I was on a mill-related errand. My courage was at a low ebb. I wasn't sure I wanted to give my tracker any ammunition.

The final rinse cycle began and I had an idea. As soon as the car passed through the last brushes, I put it into gear and took off out of the car wash, zigzagging over and down streets in an attempt to put plenty of space between my car and his. As I headed toward my new destination, I thought I'd been successful. There was no trace of the other car. Then, suddenly, in the time it took me to put my eyes back on the road, he was there.

I was growing irritated as well as frightened. Then I thought, *It doesn't matter. He'd never follow me here.*

The Oakwood Police Station is attached to City Hall, making it very convenient for reporters to pick up police and court records at the same time. The Common Council offices are housed in the same building too, making the long, low structure a municipal anthill. I steered into a space near the entrance to the police station and shut off the motor. I had to take a deep breath and count five before I could gather up my purse and walk into the building in what I hoped was a casual fashion. I didn't want to let on that I knew I'd been followed. I wanted my watch-dog to think I'd just stopped on newspaper business.

The heavy glass doors swished shut behind me and I forced myself to go farther into the office before turning around to peek into the parking lot. A smile spread rapidly over my face when I saw the blue car glide out onto the street. He'd pulled in behind me, I knew. I had heard the engine running as I'd walked into the building. Once he'd recognized where he was, he decided not to linger. Maybe I was going to report him, after all. He couldn't be sure, and that's what I'd been counting on.

I turned away from the doors, still smiling.

"Hello, Sergeant," I said to the familiar face behind the counter. "I've come for the police reports."

Five minutes later, after I'd chatted with the officer and collected the papers, I was feeling rather pleased with myself. Not only had I managed to chase off the man who had been following me, I'd also saved myself a trip to the police department. I usually get the reports from them on Tuesday.

As we talked, I wondered about telling the officer I was being followed. But I didn't wonder for long. How would it sound, after all? Especially if he checked in the lot and no one was there. I'd be branded a hysterical female and I didn't want that. In the end, I said nothing about it, keeping the conversation light.

Now, standing in the hallway leading to the Common Council offices, I wondered something else. Late on a Friday afternoon, odds were good everyone would be gone, getting an early start on the weekend. But, maybe, just maybe, Ross would be in his office. He hadn't been to his law office all day long. I knew, because he hadn't returned my call. *Unless he didn't want to return it,* some voice inside my head pointed out. I ignored it.

My low-heeled winter boots made no sound on the shiny tiles as I headed for his office. As I passed other open doors, I glanced in. All were vacant. It was almost eerily quiet, reminding me of my college days as a department-store clerk. At closing time, when the customers had gone and the store fell silent, the sensation was quite haunting. It was unnatural for the place to be so quiet. It should be filled with voices and sounds. Just as these offices should be — phones ringing, computers running, talking and laughing. But I heard nothing at all until I turned a corner into the last annex of offices.

Under one door, a sliver of light spilled out into the hallway and a distant murmur could be heard. I picked up my speed. It was coming from Ross's office.

I didn't mean to eavesdrop. I wasn't trying to be quiet and unobtrusive. In fact, my hand was raised to knock when his words reached me.

"Why won't you believe me?" he asked, in a strained and tense voice. There was no reply and I realized he was on the telephone.

I suppose I should have knocked then, or announced myself in some way, but I didn't. I stood there in the gloomy hallway, still clutching the police reports, all but pressing my ear against the door. I got what I deserved.

"Because I love you, that's why! How many times do I have to say it?" Ross said into the phone.

I took in a sharp breath, feeling as if I'd just been punched in the stomach. My ears rang, echoing his words, and I closed my eyes, leaning up against the doorjamb. I didn't hear what he said next. I was busy listening to my heart thudding in my chest.

He was in love with someone else. Why, oh why, did that thought cause me such pain? I could feel tears welling up behind my eyes and blinked rapidly to banish them. I was being silly, I scolded myself. Ridiculous! I couldn't be falling in love with someone I'd known for only two weeks. Just because we'd shared a meal and had spent that lovely Saturday together. . . . Just because when he held my hands, I felt all warm inside. And when he'd kissed me. . . .

I hiccuped a breath to prevent the sob from coming out. No need to deny it. I had fallen in love, all right.

He had too — but not with me.

Belatedly, I turned in to his conversation again. "Fine. I'll be out on Sunday. See you then." He hung up the phone and I could hear him moving around the of fice.

I knew I should leave. I couldn't possibly face him at this point. Yet it seemed as if my limbs had turned to stone, rooting me to the spot. This inaction resulted in a mad scramble a moment later.

His steps approached the door and, as I took flight, the light clicked off. I slid around the corner, back the way I had come, pausing to listen. The door closed. Keys jangled. He started to whistle.

Whistling? I thought. *After a lover's quarrel?* The tune was light and cheery, adding to my puzzlement. He didn't seem upset now, but he certainly had on the phone.

Giving my papers another squeeze — they were hopelessly wrinkled already — I set off toward the parking lot. As I wound my way through the halls, I tried not to think about Ross and what I had heard. I finally gave up the task as impossible.

I walked to my car, looking in both directions for any sign of the blue car that had followed me here. But if it was around, it was well hidden. Reaching into my pocket for my keys, I switched the papers to my left hand. My grip was poor and they spilled to the pavement.

"Drat!" I muttered, pocketing my keys again.

I squatted to retrieve the papers, but the steady March breeze began to scatter them. It took me several minutes to chase down the reports. The last one proved especially elusive, dancing gaily over the asphalt, mocking my efforts to nab it. Each time I closed in on it, my enemy the wind swooped in, sending it farther and farther away. I was ready to give up on it, thinking the police could probably supply me with a duplicate. Deciding to give it one final try, I advanced slowly, sneaking up on the piece of paper and feeling foolish.

Just as I placed my boot on top of it triumphantly, I heard my name called. I groaned.

Chapter Seven

"Hi, Lauren!"

It was Ross, all right. Cursing my clumsiness, I stood up, holding the paper away from me so it could drip onto the pavement. I forced myself to smile as I turned toward him, but I couldn't look him in the eye. Instead, I concentrated on his forehead, on the lock of dark hair that the wind had mussed.

"Hi, Ross. How are you?" Stiff words. Formal words. He didn't seem to notice.

He nodded, looking me up and down rapidly. "I'm fine. Just fine. What about you? Have a little mishap?" He gestured to my soggy papers.

"Yes," I said. "I dropped these police reports in all this melted snow. There are puddles everywhere!" My eyes scanned the parking lot. What I said was true. The lot was filled with pools of water.

"Need any help?" He reached to take the paper from my outstretched hand and gave it a brisk shake.

"Thanks, but I've got them all now."

We stood there in awkward silence. Ross shifted from one foot to the other. I cleared my throat and watched the sun send red streaks across the sky as it started to set.

"Say, um, Lauren, I was planning to go grab a pizza. Would you join me?" His voice was hesitant, as if he expected me to refuse.

I thought about how he hadn't shown up when he said he would. I thought about his not returning my call. I heard him saying *I love you* to someone else.

"I'd like that, Ross," I said. As soon as the words left my mouth, I began to kick myself mentally. He was unreliable and evasive. He'd hurt my feelings and damaged my ego and he didn't even know it. Because of him, people were threatening me and calling me names. I should run away from him, get in my car and send it careening in the opposite direction. I must be crazy to want to be around him. No, I corrected myself. I was just in love.

I risked a look at his face. He was smiling that toothpaste-commercial smile. I clenched my hand into a fist to keep from reaching out to touch his cheek. I smiled back. It felt good.

"Meet me at Pizzaville?" he suggested, handing me the paper he held.

"I'll follow you," I said. I'd been followed

enough for one day. He closed my door after I got in my car and stood nearby while I started the engine.

On the short trip across town to the restaurant, I talked to myself in a stern voice. "Remember what you heard. Remember who you are. Think about the story. Tell him about the phone calls. Don't get all mushy!"

It was hard, though. Once more, we sat across from each other, the candle in the middle casting a romantic rosy glow over the scene. After we'd ordered, I took out my notebook. But when I went to uncap my pen, he lifted it gently from my hand.

"Can't this business part wait for a while, Lauren?" He covered my hands with his own, running his thumb over my knuckles in a slow caress.

I pressed my lips together, not sure how to respond. Oh, my body was responding all right. Heart thumping, cheeks burning, knees shaking. But, verbally, I was stymied. I shrugged, trying to be casual. "Sure, Ross. Whatever you want."

He gave me a rather wicked wink. "Promise?"

I flushed, shifting in my seat and trying to pull my hands away. He held firm. "You know what I mean," I said quietly.

He gave a heavy sigh. "I think I do. You're

just here as a reporter, I guess. I shouldn't get any ideas, right?"

I didn't reply. I couldn't. My mind was whirling. He was talking as if he felt something for me, something special. And yet, I'd heard what he told someone else on the phone. What was he playing at? What did it mean?

His hand squeezed mine and I squeezed back. "You can't stop me from trying, Lauren. And I'm going to keep on trying." His voice dropped low, almost to a whisper. "I've got this feeling." He shrugged, shaking his head. "I can't explain it and maybe I'm wrong. But I feel as if there's something happening here. With us. You and me."

I nodded.

Before he could continue, the waitress arrived, bearing a large, deep-dish veggie special. After she'd served us, I used my fork to cut a piece from the slice on my plate. Before I put it in my mouth, I said, "You never came over last night. You never even called. And today you didn't call me back." I knew I sounded judgmental, but I meant to. I wanted an answer to at least one small piece of the puzzle that was Ross.

He had lifted his slice to his mouth with one hand and was in the process of taking the first bite. At my words, he frowned, chewing rapidly. I waited while he swallowed.

"Yes, I know. I'm really sorry about that too. The . . . the meeting went longer than I'd planned. By ten, I figured you wouldn't be expecting me anymore, so I went home."

"Some burning issue on the transportation committee?" I asked sarcastically.

He gave a chuckle. "Hardly that. We were talking about the new freeway, and what effect it will have on Oakwood. Kind of a yawner, actually."

I didn't believe him. He hadn't looked at me when he gave the explanation. I'd probably never know the real reason he hadn't come. I tried not to make guesses about it.

It was a relief when he asked, "What's new on the story? You told me yesterday you were getting a good response to it."

I'm sure he didn't understand why that made me laugh out loud. It was a nervous laugh, I'll admit. His raised eyebrows made that clear. Threatening phone calls at work and at home and being followed all over town didn't add up to a "good response" in my book.

While we ate, I told him what had happened, feeling pleased when he looked concerned.

When I'd finished, he said, "Lauren, that's awful! I don't know what to say. The last

82

thing I want is for you to be in any danger."

I tried to shrug off his concern, although something inside me warmed at his words. "Frank — my editor — isn't too concerned about it."

"Yes, but Frank isn't the one getting the calls."

I took another bite and chewed while I thought. He had a point. "That's true," I conceded. "But don't worry. I'll be careful. I mean," I went on bravely, "it isn't like anyone is trying to kill me."

"Not yet, you mean!" Ross blurted out. "Please don't take any unnecessary chances."

His voice was deadly serious, and our eyes locked and held across the table. I found myself thinking of other things in those seconds, marveling at the way he could make me feel without saying a word. Just by looking at me with those deep, dark eyes. . . .

"Did you hear me?"

I blinked, reluctantly coming back to reality. If he guessed I was daydreaming about him, he didn't show it.

Helping himself to another piece of the pizza, he said, "If the person who is calling you carried out his threats and something happened to you, I'd never forgive myself."

I held out my plate and laughed. "I'd never forgive you either. Trust me."

He flopped a big slice of the gooey pie onto my dish and scowled. He was not amused. "I wish you would treat this a little more seriously. How can you be so flippant about it?"

"Well, maybe it's because I don't know as much about the situation as you do," I suggested. "You were supposed to bring me copies of all the materials you had so I could look them over. So far, you know, there isn't too much for me to go on. The phrase 'whistling in the dark' comes to mind."

I let that sink in, watching him closely. He was making me nervous. I found myself looking around the restaurant for spies or balding blond men. Did Ross know something I didn't know? Something major?

"Suppose you tell me everything," I continued. "I had a few questions to ask you yesterday and I still do. Could we discuss them now?" I went to work on the pizza, waiting for an answer.

"No." He shook his head. "I mean, no, let's not discuss it here. I do have those copies for you in the trunk of my car. After we're through here, would it be all right if we went back to your place to look at them? It will be easier for me to concentrate there."

This sounded reasonable. I nodded, mentally trying to recall the state of my home. Were the dishes done? Was the morning paper still on the kitchen table? Any nylons draped over the shower curtain? Oh, well. It was too late to tidy up now.

When we arrived at the house about a half an hour later, Ross made me let him go in first while I waited on the porch. If anyone was inside waiting to beat me up, they'd have to go through him first, he said. I sat on the porch swing with my arms crossed in front of me, shivering. The temperature had dipped when the wind shifted. A steady blast of cool air whistled from the northwest and I turned up my collar. Tapping my feet to keep warm, I wondered how long Ross's safety inspection would take. I didn't think for a moment that he'd find someone waiting to attack me. Still, I admitted to myself, it was nice to have him here, taking a risk, protecting me. If I'd been alone, I knew I would have been apprehensive about entering the darkened house.

Now, instead, I was slowly going numb outside. There was only one bed to look under. Only a few closets to peek into. The basement was small. What was taking so long?

I counted to twenty, then stood up, advancing cautiously into my own home. The living room was ablaze with light. As I stepped farther into the house, closing the front door behind me, I realized all the other lights had also been turned on.

"Ross?" I called tentatively. "Hamlet?"

My cat is always waiting eagerly at the door when I come home, ready to tell me about his exciting day and listen when I talk about mine. He was nowhere in sight. Still wearing my coat and boots, I moved down the hall after checking the kitchen.

"Ross?" I called again when I thought I heard voices.

"In here." The words came from my bedroom. Puzzled, I followed the sound.

I paused in the doorway and gave a laugh of relief. My darling Hamlet lay sprawled on the flowered comforter, belly up and purring. Ross was bent over the furry creature, obligingly petting and cooing. The sight of them there, one so big and gentle, the other so tiny and trusting, touched a chord deep within me. It takes a special man, I thought as I leaned against the doorjamb, to respond so sincerely to the needs of a little cat.

"Is this all the search turned up?" I teased. "A fat cat in his lair?"

Ross grinned sheepishly. His hand moved up to scratch under Hamlet's chin. "I'm pleased to say there appear to be no prowlers in your house."

"That's a relief. Thank you, Ross. And I mean that sincerely."

He glanced up, saw I was serious, and straightened. Hamlet gave a whine of protest when his massage ended, but Ross paid no mind. In three steps, he was at my side. "I meant what I said before. I think there is definitely chemistry here, and I don't want to lose you without ever knowing where it might lead. I want you to be safe." He placed his hands on my shoulders. They were warm from the cat's body. Leaning over, he kissed me tenderly on the left cheek. "And sound." He kissed the other cheek. "For me."

With the last, his face was just a breath away from mine. Closing my eyes, I could feel him there, so close. When his lips descended on mine, I relaxed against him. He tightened his grip and I slipped my arms around his neck.

Was this really me, pulling him closer, willing the embrace to go on and on? It was as if my brain had shut down, leaving me light-headed with wonder. Some tiny portion of me knew there were plenty of problems and questions between us. But the desire for solutions and answers was not as strong as my need for his comfort, his caresses.

After a moment that seemed to last aeons and yet was still too short, he lifted his head. Rumpling up my already windblown hair, he said quietly, "This *is* special. You can't deny it." His voice was like honey, thick and sweet.

I smiled, kissing the part of him I could reach, that firm jaw with the dimple just above. "I'm not denying it," I whispered.

He put his hands on both my cheeks and tilted up my head once more so I could drown in those eyes. This kiss was more powerful and a little less tender, leaving me breathless.

"Whew!" I said, taking his hands in mine. "I think I need something cold to drink. A soda?"

He nodded silently and followed me when I started down the hall to the kitchen. While he hung our coats on the hooks near the back door, I gathered glasses and soft drinks and ice cubes.

"Better put an extra cube in my glass," he teased, coming up behind me.

My cheeks burned and I bit back a laugh. You'd think I'd never been kissed before, I chided myself. But I knew even then that I'd never been kissed quite like that in the past.

We took our glasses into the living room and settled side by side on the sofa in a cozy, domestic scene. *I could get used to this,* I thought, curling my feet beneath me.

It was hard to get down to the business at hand, when all I really wanted was to hear Ross say it was me he loved, accompanying his words with more hugs and kisses. But that could wait, I decided reluctantly.

Ross went out to his car to get the mill papers from his trunk. I cleared a space on the coffee table and he spread them out.

"Okay," he began with a sigh. "Here's the story. Everything I know, honest." His hand covered his heart. "As you have already surmised, I got this information from an employee at the mill."

I nodded. "That seemed the obvious source."

"Well, I'm not going to tell you his name because that doesn't really matter. Suffice it to say, he is in a position to know and he has confided in me."

We leaned over the papers, our heads nearly touching. There were graphs and tables and long lists of chemical names I could never hope to pronounce.

"I'll do my best on the explanations here," Ross went on, running an index finger down a page filled with numbers. "All of these substances are obvious pollutants and, as such, are regulated. There are acceptable standards for how much of each chemical can be released into the environment."

I looked at the list and felt a shiver of horror. All those awful substances, loose in our air and water. "That's horrible!" I said. "They should all be banned!" My eyes were wide with indignation.

Ross gave me a tolerant smile. "Save that for another story, you rabble-rouser. For now, just be glad there are industry regulations at all."

He pulled one of the graphs from the pile. Red lines climbed upward across it. "This shows the allowable output levels per billion." The next graph — covered with blue lines — climbed even higher. "These are the Whitson statistics. The correct ones."

We compared them. Quite obviously, Whitson far exceeded the allowable standards.

"Which chart shows the figures Whitson submits?" I asked.

Ross fanned through the papers and located a graph with yellow lines. "This one." He held it next to the others. "It clearly indicates figures below the acceptable limit. Not suspiciously or abnormally low — that would be too obvious. Just low enough to appear safe and legal."

"Pretty devious," I said. My eyes danced from one paper to the next.

For a man who didn't know much about the technical details, Ross did a fair job over the next half hour, filling me in on how the statistics were submitted and how the mill had managed to fudge them.

"We need more inspectors," I said after a while. "More people to go around making sure everything is on the up-and-up."

Ross nodded. "Yes, we do. That can be another story idea for you." He smiled fleetingly.

I shifted on the sofa, leaning back against the overstuffed cushions. "You know what my question is? Why?" I shrugged. "That may sound naive, but I guess I just am. What does Whitson gain by faking the information?"

"Well, now, Lauren, what makes the world go round?" Ross asked, sipping from his glass of now-tepid soda.

"Love? The pull of the moon?"

"Wrong, wrong. It's money. Whitson, Incorporated, gains enormous profits by not meeting the standards. They save hundreds of thousands of dollars by not bringing the mill up to specification. All that pollution-control equipment is expensive. By not using it, they save the money."

I frowned. "What about what the public-relations man told me? State-of-the-art, he said. Their brochures say it too." I picked one up, flapping it in the air.

"Doublespeak. Propaganda. Out-and-out lies," Ross suggested.

Shaking my head, I sighed, overcome with

the reality of what the papers said. Then, intruding on my thoughts came another unwelcome one. I cleared my throat and spoke without thinking. If I thought about it, I wouldn't ask, and I had to know.

"Ross, I've heard you and your uncle don't get along. I believe what you've shown me here tonight, but the reporter in me has to ask. How do I know you aren't just saying all this because you harbor a grudge against your uncle? Are you just making this up to get him in trouble?"

My question hung there between us. I held my breath, watching him, waiting for an outburst of anger and denial. Instead, his face was carefully blank, his cheeks flushed ruddy with some emotion. Anger? Embarrassment?

Tapping his foot against the edge of the coffee table, he straightened the messy papers strewn across it. When they were piled in one stack, he said, "My relationship with my uncle isn't good, that's true. I'm afraid, in a small town like this, that it's also common knowledge." His tone was disdainful, making me feel like the worst kind of gossip. "But you have to believe me when I say this is nothing personal against him. I care about this town, Lauren, about its future."

He sounded like a politician now and I squirmed uncomfortably. He caught the movement and my expression.

"Sounds silly, doesn't it? Pompous? Self-serving?" He was nodding his head, urging me to agree.

I nodded. "Yes, it does."

He stood rapidly, towering over me. "Well, I can't help that. Those are the only words I have, but they are true." He paced the short span of the living room, his hands punctuating each sentence. "I was afraid you'd jump to the easy conclusion. I figured the whole town would. It's so easy to question altruism, after all. But someone has to care about our future, or there won't be one!" He spun on his heel, returning to me. His dark eyes glowed with the fervor of conviction.

Easing back onto the cushions, he continued quietly, "My father tried to make things better in Oakwood, but he was killed before he got much of a chance. I need to continue the work he started. I seem to have inherited his concern and his drive." His lips twisted into a mocking grin. "Let me tell you, sometimes I wish I hadn't."

I picked up a pillow, fidgeting with the fringed border. "I guess I have my answer," I said without looking up. "You're either a man of your word or the best actor since Olivier."

He looked down at his clenched hands for a long moment. The clock in the room struck the hour. Hamlet wandered by, jumping up onto his favorite chair with effortless grace.

"I have no aspirations to the stage," he said. "Just for air fit to breathe and water safe to drink."

If we all had to go through life wearing hats, Ross's would definitely be white. He was one of the good guys. My heart just knew it.

Chapter Eight

The following Thursday, my second article on the mill appeared. I had written from the "what if" angle. What if Whitson's toxic emissions weren't controlled? What would the effect be on the local wildlife and habitat? I quoted a lot from cases in other cities and talked to the Department of Natural Resources for their input. I didn't mention Ross's name, of course, but I did say there were those who felt Whitson was having a negative impact on the environment.

Sources have alleged the plant is putting out contaminants in levels that exceed Federal standards, I wrote. And held my breath.

The next morning when I got to work, there was a note attached to my computer terminal. *See me as soon as you get in,* it said in Frank's heavy scrawl.

There was obviously a problem. Frank was not in the habit of issuing summonses. Usually, if he had something to say, he'd march right out of that office and blast you at your desk. If everyone else overheard, well, that was tough.

I stowed my purse in the bottom drawer of my desk and retrieved my coffee cup. If I was in for a confrontation or a lecture, I wanted to be wide-awake when I heard it. After filling the cup to the brim, I drank it half down, then topped it off again. I felt better already.

Ross and I had seen a movie the night before and then sat over dessert at the local coffee shop late into the night. It had been after midnight before I got to bed. I dreamed of dancing in Ross's arms while a balding man in an ill-fitting suit watched us from afar.

I knocked sharply on the door to Frank's inner sanctum.

"Come on in!" he called.

"Morning, Frank. I got your note, so here I am. What's up?" I sipped my coffee and eased myself into a chair.

At nine A.M., Frank looked as if he'd been at work for several hours. Shirt sleeves rolled up, tie loosened and askew, he was already rumpled. I'd never seen him any other way.

On his desk, he had a stack of manila folders. He fingered the tabs on the ends as he talked. "This Whitson thing is getting very interesting. You know I approved the article that ran yesterday. You know I stand behind you one hundred percent."

I nodded. "Yes, and I'm grateful. What's your point?"

"I received a call from Whitson's legal department late yesterday. They wanted to know who your sources were and what they had said." He gave a tight smile. "The words *libel, slander,* and *sue* were used frequently."

We looked at each other across the broad expanse of desk top. I couldn't tell if he was upset or not. I knew this wasn't good news for me. "Uh-oh," I said.

Frank shrugged. "Not necessarily, Laurie. It depends on how we play this. One little sentence in one little article and they trot out their legal bigwigs. You gotta wonder why, don't you?"

He opened the top folder. I knew it contained copies of the papers Ross had given me. The colorful, incriminating charts were a rainbow in the drab little of fice.

"If all this is true, they can't touch us. Here's the evidence. We call the cops. The end."

I gulped down more coffee. Was it really as easy as that? "I suppose if we had more proof, it would be harder for Whitson to refute it," I said.

"Naturally. Can you get it? Visit the source. See if he'll go public."

I frowned. The way Ross had talked, his

informant was dead set against coming forward. "I can try," I said. "But it won't be easy."

"Of course not, Laurie. Investigative journalism never is. You play detective and work for justice and end up with your own head on the block."

Imagery like this was not encouraging. I scowled. "Will it get chopped off?"

He pursed his lips and thought. "Hard to say. I'm not eager to find myself in a courtroom with Whitson's paid mouthpiece. That could be our financial death knell. On the other hand, if we can prove beyond a doubt the things this employee says" — he jabbed a finger at the folders — "we'd win all the way around."

I squared my shoulders, determination flooding through me on a wave of sudden and unexpected excitement. "We'll win, Frank. I promise. I'll see the source this weekend."

"And make him sing," Frank urged, lapsing into a poor imitation of a movie gangster.

"Like a canary," I replied, laughing.

"Well, go on then. Get out of here and get on it!" He waved me to the door.

"No! Absolutely not!" Ross's voice was stern and angry. "I told you he won't talk. He won't say anything on the record. He won't!"

I sighed, feeling more than a little frustrated. Reaching up behind my ear, I retrieved my pen and doodled while Ross continued to rant and rave. After a few minutes, he wound down and I jumped in.

"Will he at least see me? Off the record? Could he manage that?" I shifted the phone to my other ear during the silence that stretched between us.

"He might," Ross said at last. "I'll find out."

"Yes, do," I said, my voice short and sharp. It seemed the least he could do. "Then call me back. I'll be here until six."

I was planning on staying late at the office. Entering all the information Ross had obtained into the computer was taking me a while, but I wanted it there, safe and untouchable. I took a break around five, popping down to the deli a few blocks away. When I returned, most of the office staff was calling it a day.

If I kept at it, with no dawdling or procrastination, I figured I'd be finished by seven at the latest. Stifling a yawn, I tossed my sweater over the back of my chair and resumed my seat behind the desk.

It was creepy in the quiet office. I knew I wasn't alone in the building. The folks in the pressroom were still hard at work downstairs, but they seemed very far away just now. The clock across the room hummed quietly, as did the computer terminal. The lights in the offices around me were out. The hallway glowed softly, the red exit sign at the end beaming a weak illumination.

Time passed slowly. My eyes burned from looking too long at the electronic screen before me. When the phone at my elbow jangled, I jumped. I hadn't gotten any more threatening calls, just a lot of irritating hangups on my answering machine.

"Hello, *Oakwood Herald*," I said.

"Lauren, it's Ross. I've talked to Anthony and he's agreed to meet with you. Off the record," he emphasized, his voice leaving no room for compromise.

"That's great, Ross. Thanks for talking him into it." I wrote *Anthony* in my notebook at the top of a page. I'd keep what he told me off the record and out of my articles, but I fully intended to take notes.

"Don't thank me," Ross said with a sigh. "Thank him. He's the one agreeing to put himself in a dangerous spot."

"We're all in a tricky place now, Ross," I pointed out. "This isn't risk-free for anyone."

He gave another sigh. "Yes, I know you're right." Impatiently, he bit off the words and I could hear papers shuffling. His mind seemed to be elsewhere. I wondered where.

"When can he see me?" I pressed, pulling over my calendar.

"Tonight. He said around nine o'clock would be okay. Out at the mill."

The hairs on the back of my neck tingled a bit. Out at the mill on this cold, dark night. *Oh, Frank,* I thought, *see what I'll do for a story.*

"That'll be fine. Shall I meet you there?" I asked the question casually, hoping he'd give the proper response. He did.

"No, there's no sense taking two cars. You're still at the office now. Should I pick you up there around eight-thirty?"

I glanced at the clock across the room. I could find a way to fill in the time between. There was always work to be done. "Sure," I said. "Come to the front door and knock hard. I'll let you in."

"See you later, then."

He hung up without another word and I frowned at the telephone buzzing in my hand.

Ross was a complex man, I was finding out. Dedicated to his father's memory, his job, and his elected office, he was always busy, trying to do two things at once. And, of course, there was also the mysterious part I hadn't found the nerve to question. The part I pretended I didn't even know about. The part

I liked to think had been just my imagination. That part, of course, had to do with the telephone call I'd overheard and Ross's love for another woman.

I bit down savagely on my lip as a dark cloud of confusion descended on me. The man *I* knew certainly didn't act as if there were someone else in his life. He'd taken to calling me at least once a day. He said it was to get the latest on the story, but it seemed we talked more about everything else. The evenings we spent together were pleasant and fun, lighthearted and affectionate, always ending with a tender embrace on my front porch.

I blinked and the vision of those shared moments disappeared. People say love makes you do crazy things, and I think they're right. But, right then, I decided not to be crazy anymore.

"The next time we're together and I'm not working," I muttered, "we are having it out. I have to know where I stand."

The tricky bit would be explaining why I knew there was someone else. "I was lurking outside your door like a spy, Ross, and I heard you on the phone," didn't sound quite right. But I like to think I'm creative. I'd think of something to say.

I put that issue on a back burner and spent

the next half hour writing down the questions I planned to ask Anthony. Once I got started, the ideas flowed rapidly from my pen and my handwriting deteriorated to near illegibility.

My coffee mug stood empty at my elbow. No worse sight in the world. It would be a long evening, so I figured a cup would help keep me awake and sharp. I picked it up and went over to the pot by the wall. It was cold and empty. Whoever had taken the last cup earlier in the day had actually followed the instructions posted nearby and washed up.

I ran the cold water and reached for the can of coffee. It felt awfully light. Lifting the lid, I knew why. Empty! Now I had a decision to make. Go without or walk down the long, dark hallway to the storage room for a new can.

I looked at my cup. I looked at the hall. I started walking.

The storage room was at the very end of the hall, past the copying room, past the advertising department, even past Frank's office. It was right next to the emergency exit stairs and seemed to me, as I marched along, to be farther away than I remembered.

Of course, there was just the sound of my heels clicking on the tiles now. Outside, the wind had picked up and blow against the old building, making the windows rattle and whistle a bit. Since there was no one around to see me, I snapped on the lights in each office as I went along, illuminating the hallway enough to drive off the shadows in the corner. Not that I was afraid. No, I was just jittery. There's a difference. Honest.

At long last, I pushed open the door to the storeroom and clicked on the overhead light. It's a pretty small room — just the size of a walk-in closet or a pantry. It's filled with all sorts of essential office supplies. The coffee was stored against the far wall, up on the top shelf. Don't ask me who decided to put it there — I think it should be right inside the door.

As I stepped into the room, I heard a noise and froze. I was the only person on this floor. The only noises should be the ones I made. I couldn't even identify the sound. It might have been a creak, but that could have been caused by the wind.

I held my breath. The hand that had begun to reach up for the coffee now rested nervously at my throat. My back was to the door and I was afraid to turn around. For a full five minutes, I stood there, listening. Eventually, I reached up for the stupid coffee can, wishing I'd never begun this trek. Still, it would make a good weapon, I reasoned, hoisting the heavy, awkward container.

Turning around in the small space, I discovered I didn't like the prospect of entering the hallway.

Stop being so silly! I thought. *It's a creepy situation and your nerves are getting to you. That's all. No one is here. Listen. What do you hear? Nothing.*

Something.

I heard a whisper of movement and immediately imagined soft-soled shoes coming down the hall. Who could it be?

My heart started to pound and I swallowed back my fear, trying to be logical. Maybe Ross had come early. But how would he have gotten into the building?

Clearing my throat, I called out in a shaky voice, "Ross, is that you?"

The whisper stopped, replaced by a sound more frightening than any I'd ever heard before — a light switch being clicked off.

Slowly, the sounds drew nearer until they were easily identifiable as footsteps. As they passed each room down the hallway, the lights I'd turned on to give me courage were turned off.

My mind drew up a hundred different scenarios in those long, agonizing moments. Clutching the coffee can, I tried to picture the door to the emergency stairs. How far away was it? Was the door locked? Would I have to break the glass or sound an alarm? How long would that take?

I could move fast. I could jump out into the hall, bean the intruder with the can, leap over his crumpled body, and run for my life. Or maybe I couldn't. But anything would be better than standing here, like a fish in a barrel or a deer in someone's headlights.

I inched closer to the open door, not risking a peek out into the hall. Shifting the can to the crook of my left arm, I used my right hand to grab the storeroom door and slam it shut. Leaning my back up against it, I took several long, gasping breaths. *At least now there's a barrier between us,* I thought. Unfortunately, this door had no lock. But it wouldn't do to dwell on that fact now, I decided.

Equally unfortunate was my dawning realization that, in the process of protecting myself, I had trapped myself as well.

Whoever was out there might just stay out there all night. The minute I opened the door, I was an easy target. I might have to stay here until morning and no one would believe my story in the daylight. *Except Frank,* I thought wryly, my hand moving up to finger my still unbroken nose. *He'd believe me.*

All in all, I decided as tears began to poke and burn in my overtired eyes, covering Common Council meetings had its advantages. Deadly dull looked pretty inviting just then.

Another click sounded, just outside the door. I caught a quick breath and tensed. Every inch of me frightened and alert, I strained my ears. I could swear I heard breathing. I could sense someone's presence and knew it was malevolent.

Illogically, I knelt down, curling my five feet ten inches into the smallest possible space. Could I fit under the shelf? I wondered, backing into the corner behind the door and holding in a whimper.

From my cramped position, I could see the doorknob and was not surprised when it began to turn. I ducked my head when the door flew wide open.

The door slammed painfully against my exposed shoulder and I winced. My head snapped up as I attempted to meet my nemesis.

I couldn't see a thing. The bright, unshaded glare of a powerful flashlight was directed into my eyes. I blinked, blinded. Lifting up both hands to shield my eyes, I could make out a tall, dark silhouette. I thought I caught a glint of reflected light when I looked up at his face. He must wear glasses, I guessed.

"Who is it?" I shouted, angry at my fear and

the position it had left me in. "What do you want?" Scrambling to get my feet beneath me, I bumped my head on the corner of a shelf and winced again.

The figure remained motionless, but the light played up and down my body.

"Is this about Whitson? Did he send you? What's he hiding?"

The light stilled, shining steadily onto my face. I had his attention now.

"I won't stop asking questions," I said, bravely, foolishly. "I'm not going to go away. Go tell your boss that!" I spat out the words. My hands reached out blindly to retrieve the coffee can from where it had rolled away. I knew he saw me pick it up and lift it over my head.

"Leave me alone!" I shouted. "Get out! Get out!" I hurled the can into the center of light.

As it left my hand, the room went black. He'd switched off the flashlight. The door bumped into my shoulder once more as the dark figure left the room in a hurry.

A few feet away, the can rolled along the floor with a tinny, grating sound.

I put my head down and cried.

"Thanks for coming, Officer," I said, shaking the hand of the policeman who had promptly answered my call to 911.

He'd arrived twenty minutes earlier and made a clean sweep of the building, turning up nothing unusual, as I'd expected. I told my story as best I could, leaving out my own theory that the incident was related to the story about the mill.

I'd startled a random burglar, he had decided after investigating. The pressroom was too far away and too noisy for anyone there to have heard a prowler. I was just lucky he hadn't gotten violent.

"Will you be all right here, Lauren?" he asked, taking hold of my arm in a fatherly fashion. "Can I call anyone for you?"

I shook my head. It was nearly eight-thirty. Ross should be along any minute. I was in no mood to go out to the mill anymore, but I knew I didn't dare put off the meeting with the informant. Not at this point. "I'm expecting someone soon," I said, walking to the front door with the officer. Just outside, his squad car sent red and blue beacons coursing into the night, climbing up the building and into the trees.

The cool night air felt heavenly against my flushed cheeks. I pushed my hand through my hair.

We both looked up as we heard a car approaching fast, gravel churning under its wheels. As the automobile lurched to a stop next to the squad car, I recognized it as Ross's. He was out the door at a run, crossing the drive to gather me into his arms with a protective, welcome embrace.

"Are you okay? What's going on? Are you all right?" he asked, a frantic note in his voice. He leaned back, his arms still around me. Worry etched several lines in his forehead and his eyebrows seemed knotted together.

"I'm fine," I said faintly, gesturing to the policeman. "Ask him."

While the officer repeated the story I'd told him, I burrowed up against Ross, nestling near his shoulder, and rested my head upon his chest.

What a welcome sight he was! His arms around me communicated safety and warmth and protection. Closing my eyes, I relaxed against him, nuzzling my cheek on the soft fabric of his coat.

After the officer had gotten into his squad car, turning off the flashing lights and driving away, Ross turned to me, squeezing my arm.

"Let's go get a cup of coffee, okay?"

I shuddered and started to laugh.

Chapter Nine

We pulled into the visitors' parking area at the mill just after nine-thirty. The building looked even bigger at night, floodlit and imposing. High atop a pole near the door, the American flag fluttered next to that of Whitson, Incorporated.

I was calmer now. Like a fallen rider getting back on a horse, I'd returned to the office just long enough to gather up my purse and coat. Then, with Ross standing sentinel, I had locked up the building for the night.

"Now, remember," Ross said as he shut off the engine, "Anthony has agreed to speak with you, but he doesn't want his name brought into this."

I nodded. "I know. You've mentioned that several times."

"I just don't want any misunderstandings."

I patted his hand and gave my best smile. "Stop worrying, Ross."

Hand in hand, we mounted the steps to the front entrance and were met at the door by the man who was probably Anthony. It had to be him — he looked nervous and fidgety. As he watched us approach, I could tell that he'd love to be looking over his shoulder instead. He undid the locks on the big glass doors and waved us inside.

"Hello, hello," he said with a shaky smile.

He was average height, a bit on the lean side, and about fifty years old, I guessed, with just enough creases around his eyes and mouth to look aged, but not old. Not a speck of gray was evident in his brown hair. Behind old-fashioned horn-rim glasses, his blue eyes seemed faded and tired. He held out a hand and I shook it, introducing myself. He turned to Ross, his expression grave.

Ross matched his look and the two murmured in low conversation while I busied myself removing my gloves and studying the notices posted on the nearby bulletin board.

"Lauren?"

I turned when Ross called me, crossing the hall to join him.

"We're going to go up to Anthony's office now. And don't forget —"

"I know, I know," I interrupted with a grin. "Off the record." To Anthony, I said, "You don't have to be concerned. I'll keep everything we say here confidential."

He shrugged, wringing his hands just a bit,

and gestured toward a stairway I hadn't noticed on my first trip to the mill.

On the second floor, we turned right down a long hallway that mirrored the one leading to the public-relations department. Anthony's office was about halfway down the corridor on the left. He shut and locked the door behind us.

"Please excuse my nervousness and apprehension, Miss Sterling," he said, pulling out a chair for me. "I'm not used to espionage."

Tossing my coat over the back of the chair, I said, "Neither am I, Mr. — er, Anthony. It isn't often our little newspaper becomes involved in environmental crimes."

The office wasn't big, but there was room for a desk by the window, two chairs for guests, and, along one wall, a computer terminal and filing cabinets. Anthony took his place behind the desk while Ross and I waited.

I'm afraid I was a bit impatient with the proceedings. I'd had a terrible night, it was late, and I was tired. My entire body cried out for sleep, but the adrenaline flowing through me kept me alert and on edge. Squirming in the typically uncomfortable chair, I thought longingly of my cozy bed at home.

I took out my notebook, scribbling in the margin while Anthony fiddled with a stack of papers on his desk top and cleared his throat several times.

Ross broke the silence, saying, "We're sorry to be so late getting here, but Lauren had a rather frightening experience tonight." He glanced at me, his eyes having all the warmth of an embrace. Briefly, he gave Anthony a rundown of the evening's adventure.

As he spoke, Anthony seemed to become even more agitated. He drummed his fingers, his gaze sweeping the room. Yet he looked away when he saw me watching him.

I felt an uncomfortable stirring of suspicion. It was easy to understand his anxiety. It seemed to me, though, that he was growing frantic.

When Ross got to the part of the story when the police arrived and said I felt the incident was tied to Whitson, Anthony held up both hands and shook his head.

"Please, stop. I can explain. That is —" He paused, stammering a few times. "Tonight, at the newspaper. . . ." He looked at me, at Ross, and back at me. "I didn't mean to frighten you. I just wanted to see you. To see if I could trust you." He shrugged. "That's all."

"Wait a minute," I said, sitting forward in my chair. "Are you trying to tell me that was you tonight with the flashlight? That was you in my office?" I jabbed my pen at him, punctuating my words. Ross put a hand on my shoulder. I shrugged it off.

"Y-yes, it was. I just wanted to see —"

"You scared me half to death! Why didn't you identify yourself? How did you get into the building?" My anger flowed freely through my voice and I didn't care who knew it. Several hours earlier, I'd been cowering and terrified because this man wasn't sure he could trust me! I wondered if I could trust him. He must be crazy. "Are you crazy?" I demanded.

I was standing up now, leaning over the desk, glad it was between us or I would have punched him in the nose.

"Now, Lauren, take it easy." Ross the peacemaker was beside me, guiding me back to my chair. "I'm sure Anthony thought what he did was all right. Didn't you, Anthony?"

We sat down and stared at Anthony, waiting for an explanation.

"You have to understand, Miss Sterling, this whole business is very upsetting for me," he began.

"For you!"

"And for you, too, I know," he went on. "You see, I've been at Whitson for thirty years. I plan to retire from here. I've got a good pension. I've invested a great deal of time with this company. I don't want to leave it." He picked up a pen from a pile on the desk, clicking it on and off rapidly. "If any of this got out — my involvement, I mean — I'd get the sack. And who else would ever hire a fifty-four-year-old man who was proven traitor to his company?"

"Well, hardly that," Ross scoffed. "You aren't betraying a good person. You're exposing a bad one. It's the right thing to do. The decent thing."

Anthony frowned, unconvinced. He did set down the pen, however. "There is a term for this," he said. "For turning someone in."

"Whistle-blowing," I supplied.

"Yes, that's it. That's what I am. A whistle-blower."

"Not a traitor," Ross said. "There's a big difference."

"Tell me how all this came about," I directed. "When did you first realize something was wrong with Whitson's statistics?"

He responded better to this. He knew the facts and was willing to share. Facts don't require a value judgment.

"Actually, I'd have to say it began nearly two years ago. A long time for me to keep quiet," he said, a hint of a sorrowful smile playing on his lips. "I don't gather these statistics, you understand. The foremen in the mill do that. It is my duty, though, to report them accurately to the Federal authorities." He looked down. "I haven't done that. I've reported these lies instead." He hung his head, looking dejected.

I glanced quickly at Ross. He gave a minute shrug as if to say, *I don't know.*

Anthony looked up, leaning back in his chair. He crossed one leg over the other, bobbing his foot in a staccato rhythm. "Several years ago, shortly after a new pollution control law was passed, I noticed the statistics I was getting were consistently going down. This seemed a bit odd to me, because I knew the company hadn't changed procedures. We hadn't added any new equipment to help limit toxic emissions."

"As the law required?" I asked, scribbling rapidly in my notebook and wishing I'd thought to bring a tape recorder.

Pushing his glasses up his nose, Anthony nodded. "That's right. The first few times it happened — the lower numbers — I didn't do anything about it. I guess I thought they must be correct."

"But then. . . ." Ross prodded, his fingers knotted together in his lap.

"Then, the fourth or fifth report came and it was obviously wrong. When I got the numbers I immediately knew they were incorrect. They were ridiculously low. I went to see the engineers who gather the stats and they assured me, rather rudely, that the figures were correct. 'Don't worry about it,' they said. 'We'll read 'em, you write 'em,' one told me."

"Read them?" I questioned.

"The meters and other machinery," Anthony said, waving a hand casually.

"And did you accept that answer?" Ross asked this question, his expression intent.

Anthony squirmed under Ross's scrutiny, looking away again. I knew he felt embarrassed by his lack of forcefulness. He knew he should have come forward much sooner. *But better late than never,* I thought.

"Yes, Ross. I let it go. I'm not a pushy man. I don't like confrontations." He shook his head as he went on. "It was easier to be quiet and go about my business."

"Until?"

He looked at me when I spoke, pressing his lips together into a tight, firm line. "I went to see Mr. Whitson. We're a big company, but in some ways it's a small one. Mr. Whitson has an open-door policy and I took advantage of it. When it was time to file the statistics and they were still so low, I had a talk with the boss."

"My uncle," Ross clarified, although we all knew who was being discussed.

Anthony nodded. "And that's when I really began to worry." His eyes moved between us, drawing us into the drama. "He was very patronizing. I didn't like that. He treated me like an inquisitive child and practically patted me on the head!" Anger flared in his face and in his voice. He sat up straighter, jerking his tie into place. "He told me the lower numbers were because of the new equipment, but there was no new equipment!"

I tapped my pen against the edge of the desk. "Are you sure there was nothing new?"

"Yes," he said, nodding vigorously. "Oh, it had been purchased, but the stuff was just languishing in a warehouse. It hadn't been installed. And if it wasn't working, it couldn't be lowering emissions." As he explained, his voice became almost singsongy.

"Obviously." Ross clipped off the word. "How did you respond to Joe's explanation? What else did he tell you?"

Anthony lifted his shoulders. "He got very friendly. You know — put his arm around me, clapped me on the back. He thanked me for all my years of service to the company, and went on and on about loyalty and team spirit. He's been attending a lot of management seminars, I think." He wrinkled his nose distastefully and I had to laugh, recognizing the managerial jargon.

Ross raised a quizzical eyebrow and I realized in surprise he had never had a boss. He'd always *been* the boss.

"And — and then. . . ." Anthony began, returning to his pen and its rapid-fire clicking. He cleared his throat again, coughing a bit. "Then, my paycheck got bigger. For no reason. I'd already gotten my cost-of-living increase, so it wasn't a raise."

"He gave you money to shut you up? He tried to buy you off?" Ross said angrily.

"I fear you're right, Ross. That's why I came to you. I need advice. I need to know what to do, and I knew you would be able to help me. You are a good man."

Ross flushed and it was his turn to squirm. "Thanks, Tony. We'll get this straightened out." His hand reached for mine and gave it a squeeze.

"Does Mr. Whitson think you're content with what he told you and with the money? Does he know you're still upset and suspicious?" My pen poised over the paper as I waited for a response.

Anthony shook his head. "I haven't said anything further to him. I just took the money with no questions. He should think I'm happy."

I nodded, propping my head up in my hand, tapping my fingers against my chin.

"What are you thinking, Lauren?" Ross wanted to know.

"I'm wondering if I could persuade Anthony to let me see more of those statistic sheets," I said, looking at the man in question. "How about it?"

Anthony blinked a few times in rapid succession, as if uncertain he'd heard me correctly. I waited silently for him to make a decision.

"Well, I suppose I could," he said after a moment. "Weren't the ones I gave Ross good enough?"

"Oh, yes. They were very useful," I assured him. "But the more I have to use as evidence, the more convincing my story will be." I looked at Ross, sitting silently beside me. "And, truthfully, I want to cover myself too. I don't want Whitson to be able to refute me."

Ross nodded silently, solemnly.

"But what about me?" Anthony asked. "There aren't many places you could obtain these figures. There aren't many sources, I mean. Just the men who generate them and the man who reports them. That's me."

I shifted in the uncomfortable chair, perching on the very edge of it. I could understand his concern. He was a brave man, taking a big chance, and I couldn't promise to protect him. I could only try.

"No one will get your name from me," I said. "That's not much of a promise, I know, but it's the best I can do for now."

Anthony looked hesitant and I knew he was on the verge of saying no, maybe even calling off the whole thing.

"I guess you have to decide," Ross told him. His voice was strong and clear, urging Anthony to be strong as well. "What matters more to you — your own hide or the future of our lake and our town? What finally drove you to come forward, Tony? Were you worried about being involved in something illegal or were you concerned about the end result?"

A good question and the next one on my list. I caught Ross's eye and gave a wink of approval. He smiled faintly.

"I'm glad you asked that," Anthony said sincerely. "It makes it easier for me. Of course I didn't want to be party to a crime. I'm a law-abiding sort. But the thing that finally broke my back wasn't the money and the thought of jail. It was the idea of the pollution." His eyes clouded over, looking opaque behind his glasses. "When I thought about what all those numbers meant — in human terms — I couldn't be quiet any longer. We hear so much now about the environment, about how fragile it is, and how we must all work to protect it. How could I take money for closing my eyes? How could I allow this company to go on dumping and pretend I knew nothing?" His voice was lively now, animated by his anger. The papers on his desk top scattered as he waved his arms. He gathered them up, flapping them to punctuate his sentence.

"Yes, Miss Sterling," he said to me, tossing the sheaf of papers onto the desk with a flourish. "You'll have your statistics and your story. I'll get them for you right now."

He rose, crossing the room to the file cabinets near the computer. Fishing in his pocket for the key, he quickly unlocked the drawers and burrowed for a manila folder buried far at the back. He'd been hiding it, he explained. "In plain sight, right here in the files!" He gave a chuckle, the first I'd heard from him. It was a sharp, abrupt sound that reminded me of a barking dog. He carried the folder back to the desk, leafing through the papers it contained. He was extending it to me with both hands when Ross spoke.

"I have an idea!" he said, sounding pleased with himself. "Maybe it's silly, but it's honest. May I have that?" He gestured at the folder.

Anthony looked at me and I lifted an eyebrow. He put the folder into Ross's hands.

"Thank you." Ross took the folder with a

smile. Reaching around the side of the desk, he retrieved the metal trash bin. Ceremoniously holding the folder aloft, he dangled it by two fingers and dropped it into the basket. Then, carrying the bin with both hands, he brought it to my side. "Here you go, Lauren," he said, still smiling.

I looked into the garbage can. Just a few crumpled papers filled the bottom. The folder took up most of the space.

"Take it out," Ross urged, jiggling the can. "Go ahead."

I pulled the folder from the trash and placed it on my lap, folding both hands across it.

"There! Now if anyone asks you where you got your information, you can truthfully say that you picked it out of the garbage." Ross set the container down near the desk and dusted his hands triumphantly.

Anthony laughed again and I found it easy to join in.

"Well, that should set all your fears at ease," I teased Anthony. "Who can fault such logic?" We shared another chuckle. "Seriously, though, thank you for letting me have these papers." I patted the folder. "I'll take good care of them. No one will see them but us."

Anthony bobbed his head. "I trust you.

You're feisty. I know you'll do a thorough job."

"When did you reach this conclusion?" I asked. "When you had me cornered in the storeroom?"

"Specifically when you hurled that can at me," he replied.

I shook my head, recalling the moment and the fear I'd felt then. "I have to ask you one more question. How did you get into my office? The front door was locked."

"But the delivery door wasn't," he stated calmly. "You should speak to your boss about that."

"Believe me," I said, "I will."

Chapter Ten

By the time Ross dropped me off at home, it was near midnight. We sat in my driveway for just a few minutes, recounting the evening's revelations.

I gave a great yawn, covering my mouth with my hand and leaning my head wearily onto Ross's shoulder.

"You poor thing," he cooed, his lips brushing my temple in a gentle kiss. "You're bushed."

"And tomorrow is another busy day," I murmured. My eyes drifted shut and it took a monumental effort to prop them open again.

"C'mon. It's time you were in bed."

Cuddled together, we walked the short distance to the front door. The night air was cold and clear, the sky filled with stars. Our footsteps echoed loudly in the quiet nighttime neighborhood. I unlocked the door. While I greeted Hamlet and hung up my coat, Ross made a quick sweep through the house, peeking into the closets and the basement.

"All clear," he pronounced at last, walking with me to the front door. "You lock up behind me. I'll wait on the porch while you do."

"Okay." I smiled. His concern was so sweet. Naturally, so casually, I put my arms around him, giving him a squeeze through the heavy fabric of his coat.

His hand moved up to smooth my hair and came to rest against my cheek. When his thumb arrived at the tender spot just below my ear, I tilted my head back, inviting his kiss. His lips touched mine.

At our feet, Hamlet yowled a protest and scrambled eagerly between our legs. Ross broke our kiss, laughing out loud at the cat's antics. He hunched down and vigorously scratched behind Hamlet's ears and under his chin.

"Sorry, old man, didn't mean to ignore you," he said to the purring feline. "It won't happen again."

I think we were both sorry to see him leave that night. As his car pulled away, we stood at the window. Hamlet sat in the crook of my arm while I waved a reluctant farewell.

The house seemed so empty without him.

On Saturday afternoon, I sat at the kitchen table with the papers Anthony had given me spread out in all directions. I curled my feet underneath me and attempted to make sense of the statistics, stopping frequently to take a sip of diet cola and sigh.

When the doorbell rang around two o'clock, I was more than happy to abandon the task. Ross stood on my front porch, clad in a sweatshirt and faded jeans. He greeted me with a big smile. I wondered how he could look so rested when I knew my own lack of sleep was visible on my face.

Swinging the door wide, I gestured him in. "Hello! This is a surprise," I said, kissing him on the cheek.

He caught up my hand and raised it to his lips, pressing a kiss in the palm. His touch sent shivers up my spine. I giggled and pulled away.

"Sorry to just pop in without calling," he said. "But I was in the neighborhood. . . ."

"A likely story," I teased.

"Honest!" His grin spread, dimples deepening, and his eyes sparkled with his usual good humor. "Anyway, I thought if you weren't busy we could go roller-skating." He followed me into the kitchen as he spoke.

My eyes widened at the suggestion. Roller-skating! It had been years since I'd put on my skates, but the idea was very appealing. After sitting in one place for hours on end, I found the thought of exercise to be a pleasant one. It would do me good, I thought.

"You're on," I said, my hands already busy gathering up the Whitson papers. I tried to be orderly about it, but in the end, the papers were stuffed in the folder rather haphazardly. "Just give me five minutes to change," I requested, gesturing at my baggy sweat suit.

"You look fine to me."

I scowled. "Thanks, but I think I'll change anyway." Leaving him to play with Hamlet, I hastened down the hall to my room. It didn't take long to put on a soft plaid flannel shirt and a pair of black corduroys. My hair was a disaster, but I did my best, bending over at the waist and whisking the brush through. When I flipped my head back, the short brown locks fell in a fluffy cascade. Not bad. It took two more minutes to apply minimal makeup and I was ready.

When I emerged from my room, Ross was waiting. Hamlet had tired of playing chase-the-shoelace and slept soundly on top of the television.

"All set?" Ross asked and I nodded.

"I've just got to get my skates," I said, heading for the hall closet.

"Wait a minute. You own a pair of skates?" His voice sounded surprised and I smiled to myself.

Reaching into the dark corner, I felt around for the gym bag containing my roller skates. There it was! Bending my knees, I hoisted the bag. All those wheels made it heavy and awkward. I wrestled it from the depths and emerged victorious.

"Oh, yes," I answered Ross's question. "I've had these for years. They could probably use a tune-up." I laughed, and Ross looked stricken.

"I think I'm in trouble," he said miserably. "Are you good at this?"

I shrugged modestly. "I'm passable."

Ross held the door for me. "Well, good, because you can spend the whole afternoon picking me up off the floor."

On the front porch, I stopped, turning to look at him. "Haven't you ever done this before?"

He shifted from one foot to the other. "Actually, no. It just seemed like a fun thing to do today."

We walked to his car, parked in the drive. "You're a brave man, Ross Whitson," I said. Humming a rousing but off-key rendition of taps, I hopped in the front seat. My skates rested heavily at my feet.

The roller rink is on the edge of town. It's a popular spot on the weekends, crowded with children and their parents in the afternoon, while the teenagers confine their skating to Friday nights. The oldsters come in the evenings, when the big pipe organ plays music from the forties. As we pulled into the parking lot, my eyes scanned the rows of cars for an empty space.

"There's one!" I pointed.

Ten minutes later, we sat side by side on the long bench bordering the edge of the rink. Ross had paid our admission and was outfitted with a pair of rental skates — size ten and a half, brown with orange wheels. As I laced up my skates, my excitement mounted. Pop music boomed over loudspeakers all around us, and out on the floor kids whizzed by. Their parents generally followed at a slower pace, although some fathers seemed to be racing with their sons, winging quickly around the corners.

My toes tapped to the beat of the music and I gave Ross a good-natured poke with my elbow. "This is going to be fun!" I said.

He gave me a grimace. "Just remember, I've never done this before," he reminded me. "At least not since I was five years old."

I scoffed. "Oh, it's easy. You'll see." I stood up, towering over him as he struggled with his laces. When they were secure, he rose shakily, one hand clutching my arm. Once vertical, he gave a weak grin, shifting his feet forward and back experimentally.

"Well, this isn't so bad."

"Naw!" I agreed. "It's a piece of cake." I led the way to the floor, using the toe stop on my skate to push off. Ross followed more slowly, setting one foot down after the other, as if he were taking a stroll.

I hid my smile. This was going to be a long afternoon. It was pretty apparent that Ross was a man of his word. He hadn't skated in years.

Out on the smooth wooden floor, I spun neatly around so I could skate backward. I stretched out my hands to Ross. He looked to the left, watching for a pause in the traffic flow. Tentatively, he stepped onto the floor, looking down at his feet and shuffling.

"The first thing you have to learn is, don't look down," I said, taking his hands. "Look at me."

With an effort, he tore his eyes away from his skates, glancing up at me and back down.

I tugged on his hands. "When you do that, Ross, you throw off your balance because you bend forward. And if you get off balance —"

There was no need to finish my sentence. Ross had indeed leaned too far forward. In the time it took me to gasp a warning, it was too late. He released my hands, falling with his arms stretched out, hitting the ground in front of me with a thud.

I crouched down quickly. "Ross, are you hurt?" I put my arms around him, scanning his face. No blood. No bruises. He struggled to an upright position.

"I'm fine. Just embarrassed." I saw him look around at the crowd of skaters. His tumble hadn't attracted more than a passing glance.

"Well, everybody falls when they're learning." I showed him how to put his toe stop down as a brace — like a rock under the wheel of a car — and managed to get him standing once more. "Maybe we should go practice in the corner," I suggested. It was out of the way, against the far wall, where everybody went at first.

Ross agreed readily enough. He put his feet close together, as I asked, and didn't move, allowing me to tow him along like a tugboat pulling a barge. "I feel a little silly," he shouted to me above the music. "I mean, little kids can do this!"

I nodded. "And so can you, once you know what they know."

For the next half hour, he watched while I demonstrated, then gave it a whirl on his own. Coasting back and forth ten feet in one direction, ten feet in the other, he managed to stay out of everyone's way and stay on his feet. For the most part. Several times, my cheer of success died in my throat as his smile changed to surprise and down he went. On one particular fall, his head connected painfully with the floor. He pinched his eyes shut and sat motionless.

I crossed the distance between us in a flash. I'd seen plenty of broken bones on this floor and prayed now that Ross hadn't just become one of them. His face looked a little pale as I knelt beside him, but when he opened his eyes, he managed a smile.

Rubbing the lump on the side of his head, he said ruefully, "Help me up, Lauren. I will not be defeated!"

I put my back into it and hauled him to his feet. "Let's take a break, okay?" I suggested, pointing at the snack bar not too far away.

When he nodded, we began moving in that direction. He pushed his feet to the side, just as I'd shown him, and glided right along, bobbing now and then when his balance was off.

"You're really doing much better," I assured him.

His eyebrows knit together. "You sound like a politician, Lauren. Don't you think one in the family is enough?"

My hands dropped away from his waist and he coasted several feet past me. His words burned in my brain. They'd slipped from his

tongue so easily, so naturally, and yet what —
what? — did they mean? *In the family*, he had
said. My heart beat faster as the sentence
repeated itself in my mind. I fought to repress
a giddy smile, allowing myself a moment of
unrestricted happiness before sobering.

Ross had made it to the edge of the floor
and was safely in the snack-bar area. It took
just a few seconds to catch up to him.

"What would you like?" I asked, reaching
into my pocket for some money. "It's on
me."

We both decided on lemonade and popcorn. I carried the food to one of the booths
against the wall. Ross wasn't quite ready to
skate and carry beverages at the same time.

Once we were seated, he tucked eagerly
into the box of popcorn. "This is hard work.
I've got quite an appetite."

"Very aerobic," I agreed. "But more fun
than doing jumping jacks." The lemonade
was cold and tart, reminding me of hot
summer afternoons at my grandparents'
house.

"When we finish this, I want to go around
the whole rink," Ross said. "It's time to move
on from the bunny slopes."

I laughed. "It's definitely time to move on."

How can I begin a serious conversation here? I
wondered. But how I wanted to talk. I wanted

to ask what his comment had meant. I wanted to know there was no one else in his life. I wanted to be reassured and convinced, once and for all.

I cleared my throat. "Ross, can we talk?" My question was hesitant. If he said no, what would I do?

He shrugged, tossed a kernel into the air, and caught it in his mouth. After chewing, he said, "Sure. What's on your mind?"

I shook my head in amusement. "You're a man of many talents."

"Yes, right." He rolled his eyes. Pushing up the sleeves of his sweatshirt, he prodded me. "What did you want to talk about? Is this going to be an important discussion? Do I want to hear what you're going to say?"

I held up my hands to stop the flow of questions. "It's important to me, Ross, and I don't know if you're going to like it. I've read plenty of articles in magazines and they all say —"

"Stop right there. I will not listen to what so-called authorities have to say about men and commitment." He held my hand across the table and looked me straight in the eye.

I was filled with the urge to cup his cheeks with my hands and kiss all his questions away. The music blaring around us seemed to fade away. The chatter of other conversations receded and I felt as if we were the only two people in the building.

"This is going to be our commitment talk, isn't it?" he asked calmly.

Just like him to defuse a situation by putting it all on the table in plain view! To turn a moment of big emotional crisis into a brass tacks discussion.

I looked up at him and stopped fidgeting with the signet ring on his little finger. "Yes," I said. "I'd like it to be."

He pursed his lips and nodded. "Fine by me. Shoot."

Taking a deep breath, I said, "I really like you, Ross. I think you know that and I hope you do. I'm not afraid to say it."

I thought I saw his cheeks redden just a bit, but there was a twinkle in his eye. "The feeling is mutual. I'm not afraid either."

Well! This conversation was progressing favorably. I drank more lemonade. Now came the hard part.

"I. . . . It's been a long time since I've seen anyone exclusively," I began.

Ross dipped into the popcorn again. "Oh, me too. I haven't gone steady since high school." He put quotation marks around "gone steady" by crooking his fingers in the air.

I jumped right in. "Is that what we're

doing? Going steady?"

"I thought so."

"Are you sure?"

He put both hands flat on the table, after pushing the popcorn box at me. "Okay, Lauren. Let's have it. What's your real question here?"

I looked away. I couldn't meet those honest eyes and confess to snooping. Maybe if I weren't looking at him, it would be easier.

"Remember that day we met at the police department? In the parking lot?" Once I got started, the words came easily. I explained in a rush how I'd gone looking for him and overheard his conversation. When he started to laugh, I looked up.

"So, since then, you've been laboring under the delusion that I have another woman in my life?" He tossed back his head and positively chortled. The people at the next booth looked over quizzically and I kicked him under the table.

"Stop that! People are staring. I don't think it's so funny either."

He caught my hurt tone and immediately the laughter subsided. His cheeks were flushed from the effort and a smile still clung to his lips. "Oh, Lauren." He stood up, leaned over the table, and kissed me quickly, full on the lips. "There is no other woman, silly. I was talking to my sister, Marcia."

Marcia! I blinked. Marcia! "You were?" My heart felt lighter already.

He nodded, sobering. "I was. You see, she works with Uncle Joe. Technically, she's his boss, though she lets him run the place. She thinks the sun rises and sets around him, and she won't have a critical word spoken about him. She just won't."

"And you were telling her about the falsified records?" I guessed, covering his hand with mine. It was warm and soft, covered with fine, downy hairs.

"I was *trying* to tell her," he corrected with a sour look. "But I might as well have talked to the wind. She said I had to be wrong, that he would never do such an awful thing. She —" He broke off, pressing his lips together. After an inner battle, he said, "She accused me of trying to turn her against him, and demanded to know why I was telling her all this."

"And you said, 'Because I love you, that's why,' " I quoted.

Looking sorrowful, he nodded his head in assent. "Yes. And I do love her. I don't want to see her accidentally caught up in this mess. I don't want her to be hurt."

"She should understand that."

"She should, but she doesn't. All our lives, we haven't exactly seen eye to eye," Ross confessed. "In some ways, I think she resents me. The accident that killed our parents crippled her. I just have a few scars."

Squeezing his hand, I reassured him, "That isn't your fault."

"I know that!" he said vehemently, startling me. "But she doesn't. Or she won't believe it. She can't walk. I can. She hates me for it!" His voice grew strident with anger and I saw fire in his eyes.

"She can't hate you, Ross. She's your sister." Being an only child who had always longed for siblings, I couldn't fathom feeling animosity toward someone so close to you, someone who had shared parents and life experiences and growing up.

He shook his head, slipping his hand away to reach for his lemonade and drain the glass. "You haven't met her," he pointed out. "Someday, I'll let you have that dubious honor."

"Thanks," I said, welcoming the challenge. "I think I'd like that."

He gave me a questioning look. "Planning on playing peacemaker, are you? Well, don't bother."

His stark, bold words shook me. He truly seemed to believe his own sister didn't like him and blamed him for a situation he couldn't control. Surely there was a way he could make her understand. . . .

"Well, I certainly won't do anything you don't want me to do," I said in response to his accusation. "Perhaps if you went to her with that new information from Anthony." I shrugged. "It spells things out pretty clearly."

Ross heaved a great sigh, expelling breath from deep in his lungs. Hopelessness showed on his features. The corners of his mouth turned down and, suddenly, he looked very tired. "I suppose it's worth a try," he admitted at last, but he didn't sound terribly convinced.

"Of course it is," I said, giving a brief smile of encouragement. "Let me know if you want me to come along."

"Would you? Honestly?"

I nodded. "Honestly."

"I'll see what I can do, then," he offered. "But could we talk about something else now? Like how I'm supposed to get back on my feet and join that crowd!" He gestured to the rink, where the little kids had formed a line curving around the floor. Under the watchful eye of the skate guard, they were playing limbo, taking turns bending low under a bamboo pole held by two of the tallest children.

I dissolved into giggles at the thought of Ross teetering precariously along and joining in the game. "I'm not sure you're ready for that!" I teased.

He huffed and puffed in jest, still pouting when I got back from returning our tray. "Maybe by next time I can try it," he suggested as we skated to the edge of the floor.

All the kids were in the center of the rink, playing. That left the outer fringes free and clear. Ross dived right in, with me beside him, and we circled the floor at a leisurely pace.

"Show me some of your tricks," he said after a while. I happily obliged, ending my brief performance with an ice skater's spin.

Ross applauded as I came to a halt, spreading my arms wide for a dramatic finish. When the room stopped spinning and my eyes focused once more, my triumphant smile slipped away.

Standing at the rink's edge was the balding blond man from several weeks ago. He didn't look happy.

Chapter Eleven

Ross followed my surprised gaze and quickly looked back at me. "You know him?"

I nodded, saying quietly, "He's the man who followed you to the restaurant that day. He followed me to the police station. He's involved in this somehow."

"Oh, sure he is. That's Bernie Keeler, Uncle Joe's right-hand man," he stated matter-of-factly. "I never saw him that day at the restaurant or I could have told you then."

We kept moving, shuffling slowly around the rink floor as we talked. "So why is he here now?" I asked. "Why is he keeping such a close eye on you? On us?"

Ross shrugged. "Uncle Joe probably wants a report on my actions. Who I see, what I do. And you — well, you're the one asking all these questions about the company, so you bear watching."

I shuddered. "I don't like it. It frightens me, and I like to think I'm brave." My smile was weak, watered down by anxiety.

"I think I'll go have a few words with him," Ross stated. I reached out an arm to stop him, but he was already gone. With the smooth, measured strokes of a professional, he glided across the floor and over to the man. Dragging his toe stop, he came to a halt directly in front of old Bernie.

I stayed where I was, out of harm's way and with a good vantage point. Ross talked angrily. I saw him wave his arms. Bernie backed away, murmuring and holding up his hands in supplication. The roller skates added another four or five inches to Ross's already considerable height. He towered over Whitson's man, making an intimidating sight. As the conversation progressed, Ross wagged a finger in Bernie's face, poked him in the chest a few times, and, finally, spun on his heel, whizzing back across the floor to me.

Bernie beat a hasty retreat, disappearing through the front door that led to the parking lot.

"Ross!" I said as he came up alongside me. "You're skating like a pro!" I know I should have been concentrating on Bernie and the ramifications of his presence, but at that moment, I was dazzled by Ross's newfound ability.

"What? Oh." He brushed it aside. "It's amazing what you can do when you have to," he said, promptly starting to wobble again.

I put my arm around his waist to steady him. "What did Bernie have to say? What did you tell him? Why did you even go over there? It could have been dangerous!"

"Bernie? Dangerous?" He chuckled. "I don't think so."

"Well, in any event, he's gone now."

"And he'll stay away. I told him if he comes anywhere near either one of us, I'll get a restraining order against him."

I tipped my head to one side and thought for a moment. Since the first time I'd been followed, I had tried to be alert and watchful. Maybe I hadn't succeeded. "Do you suppose he's been tailing us all the while and we never noticed?" I asked.

Ross shrugged, as if it didn't matter much to him. "We have nothing to hide."

This wasn't much of an answer in my opinion, and I heaved a sigh of frustration. A few brisk strides and I'd picked up enough speed to make several swift turns. Forward, back. Forward, back. During my skating days, we'd called them bang-bang turns. They felt wonderful now — the speed, the spin, the self-generated breeze in my hair. I skated flat out for a good five minutes, lapping Ross several times. Finally, out of breath, I pulled up next to him.

"Feel better?" he asked, reading my mood once more.

I nodded, pushing damp hair off my forehead. "I feel wonderful. Exhausted."

A voice boomed out over the loudspeaker, "Last skate! Last skate!" Slower music replaced the pop tunes, signaling the end of the afternoon session. Ross and I edged over to the long bench off the rink floor and began to remove our skates.

It had been an exhilarating afternoon, marred only by the appearance of Bernie Keeler. I slipped my skates into my gym bag and zipped it up tight. We returned Ross's rentals to the desk.

He took the bag from my hand. "I'll carry that," he offered and I smiled my thanks. He put his other arm around my shoulders and we ambled slowly to where the car was parked. "That was fun!" he declared as the engine started.

"It certainly was," I agreed.

"Whew!" Ross let out a long whistle. He'd just read the article that would run in this week's paper. It included all the facts and figures Anthony had supplied. A sidebar would contain reproductions of the graphs. If my last article had made Joe Whitson angry, this one would make him livid.

146

Acting as my legal counsel, Ross assured me it contained nothing libelous, since the facts were documented. The newspaper's legal staff had told Frank the same thing. That didn't prevent me from being apprehensive, though.

I chewed on my thumbnail as Ross leafed through the pages once more. "I think this will bring everything out in the open," I said.

"With a vengeance," he agreed.

I wasn't sure if that was good or bad, but I found out soon enough.

By Thursday afternoon, when the ink on the paper wasn't even dry, Frank got a call from Whitson, Incorporated. They were canceling their considerable amount of advertising and informed Frank that the cost of the newsprint we purchased from them had just gone sky-high. In other words, we were to find another supplier immediately. This didn't please Frank very much. The *Herald* operates on a tight budget, with little room for extras or unexpected costs. To his credit, though, he handled it in the way I'd come to expect, blustering into the telephone and then shrugging off his anger. Never one to avoid a battle, he made sure his verbal ammunition was never fired in the wrong direction. He never passed the blame or shirked a duty.

The afternoon was full of constant interruptions, none of them pleasant. I found myself anxiously watching the clock, willing the hands to move faster. All I wanted to do was get home, unplug the phone, and soak in a tub of hot bubbles, where Whitson and paper mills and law-breaking couldn't intrude.

But it was not to be.

I got home all right and ran the tub, adding plenty of bubble bath. I couldn't quite bring myself to unplug the phone. What if there was an emergency, after all? I brought the extension into the bathroom, where it would be handy. Hamlet curled up on the rug and I sank gratefully into the water.

Steam rose, filling the room with the fragrant, flowery scent of the bubbles. The only sounds were the gentle crackle made by the mountains of foam surrounding me and Hamlet's wheezing snores.

It seemed I'd just closed my eyes when the phone jangled, disturbing our peace. With a groan of protest, I sat up, dried off one arm, and answered.

"Hello?"

"Lauren! Glad I caught you at home." It was Ross.

"You caught me in mid-bubble," I informed him, feeling lazy and sleepy from the watery cocoon.

"What? Oh, gosh, I'm sorry," he rushed on breathlessly. "But there's trouble. It's Anthony. He's in the hospital. Someone tried to run him down!"

"What!" I couldn't believe what I'd just heard and made him repeat it.

"He was here in town, running an errand. When he started to cross the road, a car came at him. He tried to outrun it and almost managed. The fender caught him and threw him into a ditch. He's got a broken leg."

For a moment, I couldn't speak. The horror of such senseless violence shook me. Suddenly, my water seemed cold and I started to shiver. "That's awful, Ross! Will he be all right? Do they know who did it?"

"No, no. It all happened so fast. Tony couldn't get a license number or even provide a very clear description of the vehicle. The police are treating it like an accident. Hit-and-run. But I don't buy that." The dread and calm in his voice made his thoughts perfectly clear.

"Someone tried to kill him," I stated, my breath coming in short, fast gasps.

"That's my opinion," Ross said. "It seems only logical."

We shared a silent moment. My thoughts whirred rapidly from point to point. "Have you talked to Anthony yet?" I asked.

"Yes, briefly. He's pretty sedated. He won't be wide-awake again until morning, according to the nurse here."

"You're at the hospital?" I stood up, toweling myself dry with one hand in a clumsy fashion. The bottom of the oversize bath sheet plopped in the water and I jerked it out, sending droplets across the room. Hamlet howled and twitched wet ears.

"Yes. I got a call from the hospital about an hour ago. Tony had given them my name. I came over as fast as I could. The police told me what they knew. Then, when I saw Tony, he said the same thing."

"Ross, is there anything I can do right now? Do you want me to come? I could be there in ten minutes," I offered.

"No, Lauren, don't. Just stay put and keep your doors locked. There isn't anything either of us can do for Tony. He's in good hands here." He let out a long, shuddering breath and I could picture him standing at a pay phone in the visitors' lounge, eyes red-rimmed with worry, his hair tousled from pushing his hands through it.

"Do you want to come over? Talk about it?" I wanted to comfort him, to conquer my own fears by dealing with his.

He gave the offer a moment's thought, then declined. "I think I'm going to go home and call Marcia. I'll tell her about this latest development and see how she feels. She's known Tony for years."

I nodded, propping the phone between my head and shoulder as I pulled on a robe. "That sounds like a good idea. Maybe this will make her listen to us."

"If she'll see us," Ross began, "and that's a big if. If she can, could you make it tomorrow?"

I pulled the phone cord behind me as I walked into the living room and retrieved my calendar from my handbag. I rapidly reviewed my schedule. "Of course," I said. "I'll cancel any appointment at any time I have to. Just let me know."

"You're a peach, Lauren. I love you." He hurried past sentiment to practicality. "If you hear any noises tonight — anything at all — call the police at once. Don't waste time looking to see what or who it is. Just call the cops."

He was making me nervous. I was already feeling frightened about being alone. I didn't need to have it reinforced just now. "Do you think they'll come for me next?" I asked. "I mean, they figured my information came from Anthony and look what happened to him. Do you —" I gulped, glancing over my shoulder into the dimly lit kitchen. "Do you think they'll take it out on me?"

"I hope not, but we can't be sure. Obviously, my uncle and his pals are getting desperate. But I never thought it would go this far, truthfully. It seems Uncle Joe cares very little about human life."

"All because he won't comply with pollution laws," I said incredulously. "Frankly, I think he's overreacting. I know the fine for noncompliance would be steep. I know the company would suffer financially. But attempted murder seems like a crazy response."

"Perhaps my uncle has finally gone around the bend," Ross said, laughing without humor. His voice had a dangerous edge to it and I could tell his mind was hard at work. "Or perhaps there's another reason for all this. One we know nothing about. After tonight, I wouldn't put anything past old Uncle Joe. He's capable of anything, Lauren. I just know it!"

I was ready to agree with him on this point, but there didn't seem to be much purpose in feeding his anger. Instead, I said, "Go home, Ross. Make a cup of tea. Calm down, if you can, and call your sister. Set up a powwow. And if she refuses to meet with us, find out when she'll be home this weekend and we'll just barge in."

"Okay. That's a good idea." I heard him take a few deep breaths. When he spoke again, he sounded better — not relaxed, but at least rational. "I'll give you a ring if she agrees to a meeting. Either tonight or tomorrow. You'll be at the office?"

"Yes. All day. You can reach me anytime."

"Lauren." His voice dropped low and soft. "I . . . um. . . ."

I smiled to myself. Those three little words stuck on his tongue now. He probably hadn't even realized he'd said them earlier. I decided to make it easy for him. "Me too." His "good night" rang in my ear as I hung up the receiver.

Anthony in the hospital. Whitson on a rampage. Marcia uncooperative and Ross caught in the middle of it all. There was no way to have a good night, I thought, reaching for the aspirin bottle. My hand shook, but just a little.

Chapter Twelve

At work the next day, the whole office buzzed with news of the scandal at the mill. My colleagues were divided on the issue. Some felt I'd performed a valuable service bringing it all to light. Others felt I'd singlehandedly doomed our entire community.

"The mill will close down now," one man muttered to another within my hearing. "All those people out of work, and for what?"

I bit my tongue, wanting to blast back, "For clean water! For a healthy environment! Doesn't that matter to you?" But, obviously, it didn't. To some folks, the bottom line was the only line that mattered. I couldn't understand such selfish logic, but decided to save my fighting strength for when I might really need it.

While I waited for word from Ross about meeting with his sister, I hit on an idea that I thought was rather clever. Maybe I've seen too many detective shows or read too many mystery novels, but I put my plan into action at once. All the information Anthony had given me was stored in my computer, safe enough unless someone stole the disk. Before last night, I wouldn't have considered that a possibility. Now, though, it seemed probable. I made two copies of the disk. I put one in a manila envelope addressed to my mother. I'd mail it with a note of explanation at lunchtime. The other I slipped in one of the blue canvas deposit bags that we use for taking the weekly profits to the bank. Corinne in the payroll department was happy to put it in the safe for me. The original papers were in Ross's hands, in case his sister came around.

I forced myself to concentrate on my other work and succeeded admirably, which came as a surprise. I did have one other mill-related errand and spent a good portion of the afternoon on the phone in regard to it.

The Federal authorities were quite interested in my story, although it took several transfers before I reached an officer who could help me. I had expected them to be as shocked and horrified by what was happening as I had been. I guess that shows my small-town naïveté. The man I spoke with, Harry Dennison, listened patiently as I told my tale.

"Unfortunately, this is not at all unusual, Miss Sterling," he said when I'd finished.

"Big businesses — and even small ones — sometimes think they are above the law. In many cases, they've gotten around the regulations for so long, they feel they should be exempt from any new ones as well."

I shook my head, imagining a lawless world where businesses and individuals did just what they pleased in a chaotic, jumbled mess.

"We'll review your information and look into this matter at once," he assured me.

I felt relieved to have shared the burden with someone in a position of authority. I could write about the mill and its violations of the law, but I couldn't enforce the laws and arrest anyone.

Harry asked me to fax him all the statistics I had, along with other pertinent information. I spent the next half hour feeding sheets into the fax machine, its rhythmic hum music to my ears. While I couldn't say I felt light-hearted, I definitely felt better. Even though Harry had told me it would take several days for the wheels to be put in motion, just knowing some legal action was on the way gave me more confidence than I'd had of late.

When Ross finally called late in the afternoon, I knew from the tone of his voice that his mission too had been a success. "Sorry it took so long to get back to you, Lauren, but it's really been a hectic day. I had several clients to see and then there were mountains of papers to read in preparation for next week's council meeting."

"That's okay, Ross. It's been busy here too."

"More flak from Whitson?" he asked in concern.

"No, nothing I've heard about. But there is plenty of mill gossip." I told him about the reactions of my coworkers and how they seemed to be divided into two camps.

"I guess you have to expect that sort of behavior," he consoled me. "I see it on the council all the time. The old guard usually shies away from change." He chuckled. "Which makes it very frustrating to be part of the new guard."

I told him about my call to Harry Dennison and he applauded the action. "Without evidence, they couldn't do anything. But now that they have the facts, we should see results in a hurry."

"How's Anthony?" I asked, doodling my version of his face, complete with glasses, onto my desk blotter. "When I called the hospital this morning, they would only say his condition was satisfactory."

"I stopped by to see him before I came in," Ross said. "He's awake now, but not in much pain, thank goodness. He looked tired, pale, and bruised, but in good spirits, all things considered."

"Could he tell you anything more about the accident?" I asked hopefully.

"No, just what he told the police. It was getting dark and it was difficult to see. He just has vague impressions of the car bearing down on him. He didn't realize it was aiming for him. He says he thought at first it was just a crazy driver, a drunk on the road. When it followed him as he swerved off the road, though, he knew it was deliberate."

"Did he tell that to the police? That he thought it was an attempt on his life?"

"He tried. The officers on the scene weren't too interested in a conspiracy theory. I talked to the chief today, though, and explained Tony's connection to the mill. I didn't come out and say he was the informant, but I made it pretty clear. He said he'd be up to see Tony later today. Chief Hately is a good egg. He'll ask the right questions."

"And any word from Marcia?"

"Yes! In fact, that's the main reason I called. She was very upset to hear about Tony. She won't believe it's related to Uncle Joe, but she does seem willing to talk." There was a pause on the line. "It's almost as if she doesn't want to believe, but knows she should. As if she knows I'm right. I get the impression. . . ." He trailed off. "I can't quite explain it."

I scribbled question marks next to the sketch of Anthony, surrounding him with them. Big ones, little ones, striped ones, spotted ones.

"No one wants to think the worst about someone they admire," I said.

"No, well, life is full of disappointments," he said in a cynical fashion. "I guess we just have to deal with it."

"That's true," I agreed. "How does Marcia plan to deal with us? When will she see us?"

I heard papers flipping and imagined Ross's desk piled high with stacks of important documents, each demanding a piece of his attention.

"I wrote it down . . . right here." More shuffling. "Sunday," he proclaimed. "Sunday afternoon at two?"

My Sundays were usually empty of appointments. That was my day to relax, curled up on the sofa with Hamlet and a good book. I knew I could make the meeting. "Sounds fine to me," I said and jotted myself a note, although there was little danger of my forgetting.

After Ross hung up, I wondered how I could fill the time between now and then. Everything was in limbo — suspended animation. Waiting for Harry Dennison to act. Waiting to speak with Marcia. Waiting, waiting, waiting for the other shoe to drop. Patience is indeed a virtue. One I only wished I possessed.

Ross and I pulled up in front of Marcia's suburban home just before two. It sat perched on a hill at the top of the block, flanked by similar old houses of rosy red brick.

"Nice place," I commented as Ross set the parking brake.

It stood two stories, with tall, white columns forming a porch that ran across the front of the house. White shutters framed the windows. A generous wreath of dried flowers hung on the carved wooden door. Several birch trees grew in the front yard and a few brave tulips poked colorful heads through the soil at their bases. The day was overcast, with a threat of rain in the air, but the house still managed to put on a cheerful face.

"Yes, it's fixed up really sharp now. It was a wreck when she bought it," Ross told me as we got out of the car. "She's got a knack for that kind of thing. A good eye for detail, you know?"

I nodded, using the black wrought-iron handrail to mount the steep flight of steps to the front door.

There was a shiny brass knocker shaped like a lion's head, but Ross opted for the doorbell instead. We could hear its echo deep inside the house and didn't have to wait long for admittance.

An elderly woman, tall and matronly, opened the door for us. Her white hair curled softly around her face. She wore a floral shirtwaist dress in muted hues that made her look like somebody's grandmother. At the sight of us on the porch, her features, which had been set into rather severe lines, broke into a broad smile. Her eyes crinkled at the corners and she let out an exclamation of delight.

"Ross, dear!" she said, holding the door wide. When we stepped into the entry hall, she spared a glance for me and gathered Ross into her arms. He had to stoop to accommodate the embrace, but did so willingly. His smile mirrored her own in intensity.

"Dolores! It's so good to see you!" He gave her a loud, smacking kiss on the cheek and she blushed prettily.

I stood off to the side, observing this obvious reunion in confused pleasure.

After the bear hug went on a bit longer, Ross stepped back, still beaming. "Lauren, I'd like you to meet Dolores Fraser." He put an arm around the woman's shoulders. "She's been part of the family for as long as I can remember. Dolores, this is Lauren Sterling, star reporter for the *Herald*, and quite a special person to me."

It was my turn to blush at the warmth of his words. I gave Dolores's hand a shake. "Hello."

"Pleased to meet you, Lauren," she said sincerely. "I'm glad to see Ross looking so happy, and I'll bet you're part of the reason." She reached up to pat his cheek. "I used to look after the children when they were little and I've stayed on to help Marcia." Her words seemed to spark her memory and she rushed on, "I'll just go see if she's available. I know she is expecting you."

Ross nodded. "We'll wait in the library?" he suggested.

She waved us in that direction, and we walked down the polished wood hallway to a cozy room lined with bookshelves. A low fire burned in a stone hearth in the corner, taking the chill from the room. I took a place on the chintz window seat. Ross roamed the room, pausing and turning his head to read book titles.

We were both nervous. I showed it by saying nothing and picking at the polish on my fingernails. Ross whistled a staccato tune in a way that would have been irritating had it gone on for very long.

Inside of five minutes, though, the creak of the wheelchair could be heard in the hall. I watched Ross's face as his sister entered the room. His brows were knit together again, but only for an instant.

"Marcia!" He moved to her side, bending low to drop a kiss on her cheek. Gripping the handles on the chair, he pushed her farther into the room, placing her by the fire.

I could see the family resemblance immediately. Marcia too had thick, dark eyebrows that served as a good mood indicator. They were raised now, arching in question as she regarded me.

"I'm Lauren Sterling," I introduced myself, extending a hand.

She hesitated just long enough to make me feel awkward, then gave my hand a firm clasp. The muscles in her arms were quite strong from pushing the wheelchair. I didn't let my smile slide as the bones in my hand were pulverized.

"Pleased to meet you," she said automatically. Her voice belied her words, sounding harsh and uninviting.

I glanced over her head to Ross and he gave me a reassuring grin.

"I'm glad you agreed to see us, Marcia," he said, pulling up a tapestry-covered wing chair and sitting down. "What we have to

163

say is very important."

Marcia heaved a sigh and squirmed a bit, fidgeting with the soft bow tie of her lavender blouse. She tossed her head, with its sleek crown of short, dark hair. The perfectly cut bob fell gracefully back into place. "I've said I'll listen to you, Ross, but that doesn't mean I'll believe you. It will take an awful lot more than just your word to convince me Uncle Joe's doing something illegal. It would be just like you to say something bad about him. Everyone knows you hate each other." The chip Ross had warned me about was firmly mounted on her shoulder.

Ross wisely chose to ignore her jab. "You won't have just my word. You'll have evidence, which Tony nearly paid for with his life. Surely you can't think Tony is prejudiced against Uncle Joe too!"

Marcia raised her shoulders, shrugging by way of answer.

Clearing his throat, Ross opened the briefcase containing the original papers we'd received from Anthony and began his presentation. With me providing additional commentary, we gave her all the background information we possessed.

"You know Tony is an honest man," he prodded Marcia until she nodded her head curtly in agreement. "He couldn't keep quiet about this." He shook the papers clutched in his fist. "And neither can we."

Marcia rubbed the heel of her hand against her eyes, then snatched the papers away from her brother. "May I?"

"By all means," he said.

While she studied the statistic sheets we had painstakingly explained only minutes earlier, Ross came to sit beside me at the window.

"What a view, huh?" he asked, placing his hands on my shoulders and kneading the tense muscles.

I could only agree. We were so high up on the hill that the view from the window was one of treetops and roofs leading down to the lake. The houses were mere specks of color amongst the green, but it was the lake that dominated the scene. Today, with the sky hanging low, the water was slate-gray. White foam showed in a flash as each wave crashed against the breakwater.

I pressed my nose closer to the glass, thinking of lake breezes in the summertime, when the windows would be open to the fresh air. When Marcia spoke, I came back from my daydream.

"I must say, you've certainly done your homework. If all this is true, the mill could be financially ruined, you realize."

Ross shrugged. "That's hardly my fault or my intention, Marcia. The mill has a steady clientele and a healthy account base. Surely you could deal with any momentary setbacks."

Marcia's eyes were dark with astonishment as she picked up on Ross's intention. "Are you suggesting I throw Uncle Joe out of the business?"

"Not as a shareholder, just as an administrator. It's an idea you should think about," he said calmly. "I can't bring it about — I don't own a piece of the mill. But if I did, I wouldn't allow an incompetent man near the helm, damaging my investment and my good name."

He struck a chord there. Marcia fell silent and thoughtful. Ross knew his sister well. He knew Whitson, Incorporated, was the most important thing in the world to her, and he knew she'd do anything necessary to protect it. I could practically hear the wheels turning in her brain as she thought, drumming her fingers on the arm of her chair.

"I'll tell you what I'll do," Marcia began slowly, still thinking. "I'll do a little checking on my own at the office on Monday. I think I can ask a few discreet questions here and there without arousing too much suspicion." She leveled a sharp look in my direction.

"Although you and your articles already have everyone looking over their shoulders." A brief hint of smile suggested a dimple in her cheek. Turning to Ross, she went on, "So let me see what my own little investigation reveals. I think I know just which rocks to overturn." Her eyes narrowed dangerously and I was glad I wasn't one of those rocks.

"Call me, will you?" Ross pressed her. "The minute you learn anything."

Marcia tipped her head to one side, watching Ross in an appraising way. "Just can't wait to nail Uncle Joe, can you?" she asked, a bitter note tainting her words.

When Ross opened his mouth to respond, I put my hand on his arm. "I'm sure Marcia will be in touch," I said, at my diplomatic best. "I'm also sure she has other things to do this afternoon." I inclined my head toward the door.

"Right. Well, I'll just wait to hear from you then," Ross said, stopping at his sister's wheelchair to kiss her cheek once more. After a few more farewell pleasantries, we were on our way.

Back in the car, I asked, "Do you think it was a good idea to leave the papers with her?"

Ross put the car in gear and gently accelerated. "I don't see why she shouldn't have them. We have copies. And besides" — he sent a quick glance my way — "if anyone from Whitson decides to go looking for them, they'll never think to look here!" He gave a laugh, but I didn't see what was so funny.

"Because you two don't get along?" I clarified and Ross sighed, rolling his eyes.

"Yes. Given our past relationship, no one would ever guess we'd be in cahoots. Although I'm not convinced we are. Time will tell," he decided.

The words had an ominous ring.

Chapter Thirteen

On the ride back to my house, I mulled over Marcia's supposed feelings toward Ross. He had said she resented his healthy body because she was disabled. I could understand that, if I tried. If I put myself in her place, I could see why she would be envious of anyone who was unafflicted. This didn't strike me as a healthy attitude, of course, but a completely human one, nonetheless.

"I know this is none of my business," I began hesitantly, "and you can tell me not to be nosy if you'd like, but I was just wondering. . . ."

When I paused, Ross smiled and, without taking his eyes off the road, said, "What was your reporter brain wondering, Lauren?"

I shifted in my seat, trying to face him, but restricted by the safety belt. "Why does Marcia seem to think you have it in for your uncle? She seemed so sure you were doing all this just to get back at him."

Ross nodded, sighing softly at the troubles

his sister gave him. "It's part of her theory that I'm the one with problems. She's managed to convince herself that the reason Joe and I don't get along is because I harbor a secret desire to run the mill."

"What?"

"I know. It's crazy. I signed away my interest in the company years ago and I've never regretted it. I wanted nothing to do with it, then or now. Marcia feels otherwise. She firmly believes I'm sorry I walked away from the prestige and the money the mill could bring. It's just lunacy, and I hope someday she'll realize she's been wrong about me all these years."

His words were logical and straightforward, but in his voice I could hear the pain his sister's attitude caused him. When he spoke again, he confirmed my deduction.

"All I've ever wanted is for her to understand me! If I could give her my legs, I would have done so years ago. I don't want her to suffer physically or emotionally, and yet I know she does. Sometimes, Lauren" — his hand groped for mine and clasped it tightly — "sometimes, at night, I lie awake wondering what our lives would have been like if the accident had never happened. If Mother and Father had been around for us as we were growing up, so many things would have been

170

different." He smiled, shrugging in a cynical way. "We all would have lived happily ever after in the enchanted forest," he said, poking fun at his dream.

"Well, it's true that nobody's life is ever idyllic for long," I said. "We all dream of happiness that seems too elusive. It isn't silly to dream, though." I gave his hand a squeeze. "Dreams are . . . the fuel we use to get through everyday trials," I expounded, warming to my theme.

Before I could wax poetic much longer, Ross's snort of laughter cut me off. He gestured expansively with one arm, saying in theatrical tones, "Dreams are the safety nets on the trapeze of life." He dissolved into great hoots of laughter.

I couldn't be offended. It gave me a warm feeling to hear him laugh with such pleasure, to see his eyes twinkle as he looked over at me for my reaction. Screwing up my face, I stuck my tongue out, setting him off again. He was still chuckling as he pulled in my driveway.

On Monday night, the Common Council held their monthly meeting. The reporter who usually attended this spine-tingling event was down with a recurrent head cold. When Frank asked if I'd cover it, I had no trouble saying yes. It wouldn't be the first time I'd seen Ross wearing his alderman hat, but I welcomed the opportunity anyway.

Ross and I had dinner together and set off for City Hall. The transportation committee met first at seven o'clock. Ross hadn't heard from Marcia and when he took his place on the dais, he looked tired and harried.

The meeting was a long one, filled with all the minor altercations I'd come to expect when politicians gather together. As tempers flared over yet another minor point, Ross sent me a visual SOS. I did my best to look reassuring and comforting, attempting to put the warmth of my love for him into my eyes. I must have succeeded to some degree, because he smiled and closed one eye in a conspirator's wink.

Much later, as we drove home, he lamented the friction on the council. I let him complain, knowing he needed to let off steam. After ten minutes, he ran out of words and sighed into silence.

"Got that out of your system?" I asked. I put my left hand on the nape of his neck and massaged gently.

He gave a sigh of pleasure. "Oh, Lauren, you always know just what to do," he crooned, his voice low and husky.

I laughed. "I hope I'll always know."

He turned into my driveway and put the car

in park. After unsnapping his seat belt, he torrid to me, gathering me close. Tangling his hands in my hair, he said, "Oh, I think you'll manage."

When his lips touched mine, I closed my eyes, allowing myself to relax in his arms. Clasping my hands behind his neck, I returned his embrace. My limbs seemed to tingle with a tender form of excitement and I squirmed a little closer. As the kiss ended, we pulled away from each other and I moved my hands to softly touch his face. His skin was warm and smooth beneath my fingers.

"Mmm," I purred, feeling cozy and sleepy. I rested my cheek against his for a moment, then moved back so I could look into those deep, dark eyes. "I love you, Ross Whitson," I declared, my lips just a hairsbreadth from his. He didn't have a chance to reply.

Several evenings later, Ross and I were engaged in a rousing match of Chinese checkers at my house when the phone rang. We didn't mind the interruption — Hamlet had declared the game over moments earlier by walking firmly across the game board, scattering marbles over the living-room rug.

While Ross gathered up the marbles, I answered the phone. "Hello?"

"Hello, is Ross Whitson there?" The voice

was female and breathless, speaking in a rush.

I frowned. "Yes, he is. Who shall I say is calling?" I fished.

"It's his sister, Marcia," she said curtly. I should have guessed.

Covering the mouthpiece with my palm, I stretched the phone cord around the corner from the kitchen into the living room. "Ross, it's for you." I held out the receiver to him. "It's Marcia."

Our eyes locked and I knew we were both wondering what she had to tell us. He deposited the marbles in their container and got rapidly to his feet. I stood at his elbow and listened while they talked.

"Hello, Marcia," he greeted her. "What's up?" The casual phrase wasn't matched by his serious expression. For the next several minutes, he nodded his head a lot, giving brief replies to her comments. "Yes, yes, I understand. He told you this? Yes. Yes. Can he prove it?"

I thought I would go mad with frustration as I listened, shifting my weight from foot to foot in a nervous jig.

At last, Ross said, "Of course we'll meet you tomorrow. We'll be at your place at seven-thirty sharp. See you then, and —" he paused, changing his tone from businesslike to comforting. "Don't worry. It'll be all right.

But keep a low profile, will you? Maybe you should stay home from work tomorrow."

I could hear Marcia's squawk of disapproval from where I stood and Ross hurried to qualify his suggestion.

"It was just an idea. To keep you out of harm's way. I know! I know you can take care of yourself. I didn't mean to imply —" Her response cut him off again and he rolled his eyes in exasperation. "Right. Well, whatever you think. We'll see you tomorrow. 'Bye."

"Kind of touchy, huh?" I asked as an understatement.

"Kind of," he agreed. Shaking off the lively end of their conversation, he put an arm around me and we moved to the sofa. "She had plenty to tell me, though. I think you'll be surprised. I know I was."

I leaned toward him. "What?" Hamlet jumped up beside me and I absently began to stroke his downy coat. At least someone didn't have any problems, I thought as the sound of his purr reached me.

"Marcia said she asked a few questions at work today. 'Called in a few favors,' she said, so I can just imagine the eager response she got."

Nodding, I said, "She does appear to be a very direct sort of person — won't take no for an answer."

Ross lifted an eyebrow in agreement. "Anyway, she learned Uncle Joe set up a special account several years ago when it became clear that more and more pollution control laws would be implemented. It's called the Environmental Fund, and a portion of each year's profits is deposited directly into it."

I was taken aback, surprised and befuddled. "Well, that's commendable. Smart too. How come Marcia just found out about it now?"

Ross put his hands to his temples and shook his head. "Lauren, Lauren, Lauren. Your innocence is charming. And amazing."

"What do you mean?" I challenged, confused.

"Almost no one knows about this so-called fund. Uncle Joe has it rigged to look like a legitimate account to the bookkeeping department and the IRS."

A light bulb went on over my head and began to glow. "But it's not legitimate at all!" I exclaimed.

"That's right. Marcia thinks it must be some kind of slush fund. But if you ask me, embezzling is the word for it."

"Wow!" My breath came out in a gasp and my eyebrows shot up under my bangs. I leaned back against the sofa cushions and attempted to absorb everything I'd just been told.

When slipped into the bigger picture, this revelation gave dire new implications to the story. I wasn't sure I was prepared to follow where it could lead, but Ross's legal mind was already way ahead of me.

"The ramifications of Marcia's information are awfully far-reaching," he pondered aloud. He tapped his finger against his chin and thought.

I wisely decided not to interfere in the process and spent the next several minutes mentally constructing the lead paragraph for the article I'd write after tomorrow night's meeting with Marcia.

Ross's fingers drummed more insistently until finally he sprang off the sofa and began pacing and mumbling.

Hamlet, still sitting beside me, watched him closely, his head turning this way and that like a spectator at a tennis match. After ten minutes of near silence with Ross roaming the room while I sketched notes on a handy sheet of newspaper, he stopped in front of me.

I lifted my head to look up at him as he said, "You know, I kind of feel sorry for Uncle Joe." He sounded serious and mournful and I knew his emotions were genuine. "I mean, the misguided old man is in serious trouble now — with Federal authorities for the pollution problem and, probably, with other authorities for stealing money from the mill." He shook his head. "Greed is an awful thing, Lauren. My uncle could have done so much for Oakwood. He could have done all the things my father had planned. But, instead, he did what was best for only himself, never minding that it was against the law."

"This must be very hard for your sister," I said.

"Yes, it will be, once she truly believes it. I get the impression from what she said on the phone that she still thinks it's just some irregularity or bookkeeping error."

"Even with the evidence staring right at her?"

"Even so."

I thought a bit more. Whitson had threatened and followed me. He'd nearly killed poor Anthony. He was a dangerous man. "I think we should go to the police right now. I think we should tell them what Marcia has learned and let them deal with it. That's their job, after all." I spoke firmly, tamping down the little voice inside me that was quaking with fear. I didn't want to wait for Whitson to make another move against one of us.

"No," Ross said just as firmly. He sat beside me. "We can't go to the police about the suspected embezzling just yet. For one thing, we haven't seen the evidence. All we've heard is the bit Marcia told me. We'd have to be sure to bring in the police."

"But, why? Why can't we let them do the digging?" There was no good reason I could think of.

Ross sighed. "I guess I'm being selfish." He rubbed his eyes. "I feel like. . . . If my uncle really is stealing, I don't want to find out secondhand. I want to know before it's common knowledge."

I scoffed. "Oh, Ross, that's silly. I'm sure the police would tell you immediately whatever they found out. And besides, if it is true, as you suspect, you won't be able to keep it quiet. It'll be all over town in no time. You know that." I gave his hand a pat.

"I know that," he agreed reluctantly. He turned, taking my hands in his and looking intently into my eyes. "How about this? How about if I promise you that tomorrow night, right after we talk to Marcia, we go to Chief Hately and tell him everything we know. Would you agree to that?"

I hemmed and hawed, unsure, finally deciding that another twenty-four hours wouldn't make much difference at this stage of the game. "All right, it's a deal." I held up one finger and wagged it in his face. "But I want to go on record saying we should see the cops now!"

He flashed a smile. "Duly noted, Miss Sterling." Glancing at the newspaper covered with notes, he asked, "What have you got there?"

"My story," I said simply. Clearing my throat, I read him the few lines I had written.

Time is a funny thing. It can go by so quickly, as it does when you're on vacation. But it can also go by so slowly, like when you're at the dentist. All the next day at work, I felt as if I were in the waiting room at the dentist, knowing it would soon be my turn so I couldn't go home, but not wanting to stay, either.

Knowing that, come evening, we'd hear the details on the Environmental Fund and then go to the police, I was nervous and on edge. I drank more coffee than I should have, and the caffeine made my heart race. Each time the phone rang, I expected the worst. A threat, bad news, some tragedy out at the mill. But it was always just business as usual.

At lunch, I called Ross's office and we reassured each other in low tones. "I'd like to tell Frank all this," I confided, tucking the phone against my shoulder. "He's at a meeting right now, but he should be back before three."

"Do you think he'll be able to help?" Ross sounded doubtful.

I shrugged. "I'd just feel better bouncing this off him. He's had plenty of experience in matters like this, you know."

There was a pause on the line. "Well, if you want to," he said at last, "go ahead."

We solidified our plans for the evening. Ross would pick me up around seven. It was hours and hours away.

Later, after Frank's return, I sat in his office and told him the latest. To my surprise, he agreed with Ross. "Talk to the sister, then to the cops. Whitson isn't about to bump off his nephew or a reporter tagging his heels. It would be too obvious and too dangerous. I think you're safe, Lauren."

I was getting just a little tired of people telling me I was safe when every cell in my body shrieked otherwise. Still, Frank was a person I trusted. His judgment meant a lot to me and I had no reason to question his motives. When I stood up, I gave him one of my best smiles. "I hope you're right about this."

He put his feet up on the bookcase and crossed his arms behind his head. "I've been right so far."

If this was meant to calm me and soothe my nerves, it did not. It sounded like a brag, waiting to be jinxed.

"So far," I repeated, lifting an eyebrow.

"Listen, if you want to give me a call after the meeting and fill me in, please do. You have my home number?"

I nodded. "Maybe I'll do that." I returned to my desk and began the long, long wait for seven o'clock.

Chapter Fourteen

I bolted out the front door when Ross's car pulled in the drive, not even giving him time to turn off the engine. My notebook was in my purse, and I'd had the foresight to bring along my little tape recorder too. I bounced onto the seat beside Ross and leaned over for a kiss.

The smile he gave me was bemused. "You certainly look enthusiastic," he said as I fidgeted with my purse.

I smiled. For once, his ability to read my mood was seriously off the mark. "Actually," I confessed, "I just want all this to be over. It may be the biggest story of my career, but right about now, I can honestly say I'd be happy to type the words 'The end.' "

He laughed, suggesting, "How about 'They lived happily ever after'?"

"Even better!" I concluded, nodding my head energetically.

Tonight, the drive to Marcia's house went quickly. Ground lamps in the bushes out front gently lit the walkway. A brass lantern hung near the door, bathing the porch in welcoming light.

While we waited for Dolores to answer our knock, Ross leaned over and kissed me rapidly but thoroughly. At my startled look, he said simply, "A kiss for luck." Before I could respond, the door opened and our evening's adventure began.

We met once more in the library. Marcia was already waiting for us near the window, casually attired in jeans and a hand-knit sweater. She wheeled forward to greet us.

"Ross. Lauren. You're here!" she exclaimed, as if our presence surprised her.

Ross checked his watch. "Right on time, Marcia." He raised an eyebrow, wordlessly asking a question.

Marcia knotted her fingers together in her lap. "I . . . I was worried about you. About whether you'd come and what I'd do if you didn't." Her voice shook slightly, betraying her. Heavy creases marred her forehead as she frowned.

Ross went to her side, leaning down so he could look into her face. "I know this all comes as a shock to you, just as it has to me." He covered her hand where it rested on the arm of the chair. "But we'll figure it out together and we'll fix it as best we can."

He could have been a little boy assuring his kid sister that he could mend a broken doll. Marcia responded to him in a similar way. There was a softening around her mouth and the creases on her brow melted away. She looked years younger, and much different from the hard-as-nails facade I had seen her project earlier. I did my best to melt into the woodwork while the siblings talked. It was Marcia who finally remembered my presence.

"Thank you for coming, Lauren. I appreciate all the time you've spent researching our . . . our problem. I just hope it comes to a satisfactory ending." She pressed her lips together, making a fierce face as she battled inner conflicts. "Although how there can be any satisfactory conclusion is beyond me."

I pulled up a chair and sat down, and Ross did the same. I had my notebook open on my lap and my little tape recorder at my feet. When I gestured to it, Marcia nodded her approval and I switched it on.

Ross leaned forward to his sister and said, "Tell me everything. Right from the start. Who did you talk to? What did they tell you?"

Marcia sighed, using the moment to gather her thoughts before plunging ahead. "As I told you on the phone," she began, looking from Ross to me and back again, "I did a bit of snooping at the office yesterday. It wasn't as difficult as you might expect, either, because, after all, I am a Whitson and I am the boss too." She smiled in a manner that was not at all unpleasant. "I'm not above using my position if it suits me, you know."

"I know," Ross replied in a droll tone. "Go on."

"Anyway, I talked to a few of the department heads who have always been helpful in the past. We have kind of a you-wash-my-back-and-I'll-wash-yours deal," she explained. "They didn't know much, which isn't too surprising, but they had heard a few rumors. The rumors had never made it to my door and they were very vague."

"How vague?" I asked. "They must have led you somewhere."

"I'll say they did!" she exclaimed. "Whitson, Incorporated, has a special office set up at the mill for an organization known as the Expansion Committee," she explained. Ross nodded, as if this were old news. At my puzzled look, Marcia clarified, "All perfectly legal and aboveboard. It's been around for years. Its goal is to plan the future of the mill and make long-range projections on trends and expenses. Keep the mill competitive. Understand?"

"Yes," I said. My pen hovered above my paper. "Who is on this committee?"

"At various times, it is made up of different individuals on the board of trustees. They rotate the assignment. It goes with the territory."

"But where does the Environmental Fund come in?" Ross broke in impatiently.

"I'm getting to that!" Marcia snapped. "When I talked to Fred in Development about toxic-emission controls, he mentioned this fund and how the money in it was supposed to be used for improvements, but his department never saw any. I pressed him" — she smiled — "in my gentle way. I asked him what fund he was talking about. He clammed up and turned red as a beet. That really set me off!" Her eyes, so like Ross's, blazed with fury.

Ross said, "You were totally in the dark? You have never heard word one about this so-called fund?"

Marcia was shaking her head. "No! I never heard a whisper!" She held up a finger. "My guess is Fred heard it by accident, judging from his guilty reaction."

"But who set it up?" I persisted, still lost.

Marcia grinned, resembling a certain cat after a successful hunting expedition. "Let me tell you how it must have worked. The trustees are all on plenty of committees — more than are really necessary, actually.

Some of these committees never even meet. They only exist in theory, on paper. To look good."

"And the Environmental Fund grew out of one of those nonexistent committees?" I guessed.

"That's right. The fund was set up over five years ago! It was a particularly turbulent time at the mill, personnel-wise. If I remember, we'd lost a few board members to retirement, one died, and there were several months when committees were virtually memberless. The title was there — Expansion Committee — but no one was in charge. No one was responsible. No one was accountable!" Her voice went up, urging us to draw our own conclusion.

"Uncle Joe saw a golden opportunity to . . . increase his holdings," Ross stated.

Marcia's face fell. She'd become animated while telling her story, but now we'd reached the sticky part. The disagreeable part. "Yes," she said quietly, her voice barely reaching us. "I wanted to give him the benefit of the doubt, you know. I wanted you to be wrong about him, but now that I have all the facts, I have to face the truth."

"I'm sure he wasn't entirely alone in the idea," Ross pointed out. "There must have been others in on the scheme."

"But it's still a scheme," Marcia said, her voice breaking. She shook her head and her glossy hair swung. "I can't bring myself to totally believe it. In my head, I know it's true, but my heart wants to deny it."

There was nothing either of us could say to ease her pain at her uncle's betrayal. We exchanged a sympathetic look.

"I trusted him!" Marcia railed. "I took his side against you, Ross. I know I've always blamed you for things in the past when maybe I shouldn't have. This time too. I thought you were the shifty one — the one out to cause trouble for the mill. Now, it turns out, Uncle Joe is responsible for our problems."

"There seem to be plenty of those," I muttered as I wrote and Marcia swiveled to look at me.

"Yes. And it's all so clear now. The pollution violations. The Environmental Fund. The attacks against you and Tony." She ticked them off on her fingers.

"I always thought his reaction to the newspaper articles was out of proportion," I said, wagging my pen in the air. "The threats were frightening enough, but the deadly attack on Anthony was ruthless!" I shuddered involuntarily at the memory. "At least now I can understand why his response was so violent," I continued. "He must have realized that as soon as someone began examining the Federal toxic-emission standards and found they were being falsified, they would start poking into other matters at the mill. Whitson figured he'd save the mill money — and line his own pockets — by not complying with the Federal laws. Instead, he just attracted a lot of unwanted attention."

"And he's about to get a whole lot more," Ross commented wryly, explaining to Marcia that the Federal environmental authorities had been notified and would soon be acting on the issue.

Marcia let out a groan. "This is so overwhelming! It was awful enough to think Uncle Joe was totally disregarding our community by allowing the dumping and lying to the government. But now to find out he's been skimming thousands from the mill profits!" She broke off, shaking her head in amazement.

Ross shifted in his chair, edging a little bit closer to me. The tape recorder at our feet fell over as he bumped it. Absently, I set it back up, flipping the tape over to a clean side.

Giving Marcia an encouraging smile, Ross prodded, "Tell me about being a detective. You said Fred mentioned the fund to you originally, but how did you trace that remark back to the Expansion Committee?"

Marcia straightened her shoulders and batted her eyelashes, looking very pleased with herself. "It was a snap!" She made the accompanying gesture with her fingers. "You know Uncle Joe is a meticulous man."

Ross nodded. "I thought the phrase you preferred was 'pack rat,' " he teased.

"Semantics, Ross," she dismissed him. "I thought if I could rummage through his files, I might find something . . . well. . . ."

"Incriminating?" I supplied, scribbling in my notebook.

"Yes, that's right," she hurried on. "So I waited until I knew he'd be at the Chamber of Commerce meeting and then I rolled on down the hall to his office."

"And just let yourself in?" I asked.

Marcia shrugged. "More or less. I told his secretary Uncle Joe had asked me to compile a report on Whitson's efforts to control pollution." She winked at me, looking suddenly impish. "I told her it was for a report to the Board in response to your articles in the *Herald*."

I pursed my lips. "Very clever."

"Thank you. Anyway, that was enough to satisfy her curiosity. She didn't ask any more questions, just rushed right over to open the door for me, offering to retrieve any files I couldn't reach. Some people overdo it around those of us who are physically challenged," she told me with a sigh. "They overcompensate out of guilt or something, I guess." Her shoulders lifted once more and she resumed her story. "I let her dig out the folders, then I went to work."

"And it was all there in black and white?" I asked incredulously.

"Let's just say I only needed one look to know several things. First off, the Environmental Fund is phony. Second, Uncle Joe is sharp as a tack."

Ross and I exchanged a look, then we both spoke at once.

"What did you find?"

"Did you make copies?"

"Copies? No. Why should I?" Ross's mouth began to drop open, until she added, "I brought the originals home with me." She wheeled rapidly over to one of the bookcases and pulled out an oversize atlas. With a flourish, she opened the cover and reached inside, producing a sheaf of papers. "I plan to put these in my safe tonight, but I thought you might like to take a look at them first." She handed the evidence to Ross. "Take a look at the names of the original incorporators," she said. "I think you'll recognize them."

I looked over Ross's shoulder as he flipped

to the back of the document, my eyes rapidly scanning the sheets. There were three signatures on the last page. Joseph Whitson I knew, but. . . .

"Who are Barney and Lilly Grantchester?" I asked, turning to Ross for an answer.

Slowly, sounding stunned, he replied, "Barney was our dog."

"And Lilly was the canary," Marcia put in.

"Grantchester," Ross explained, "was our mother's maiden name."

For the space of a heartbeat, no one spoke.

"These are dummy documents!" I nearly shouted. "Your uncle made them up. He must have been expecting trouble."

"Or just wanted to be prepared if anyone asked questions," Marcia added. "Clever of him, really."

"This was a dangerous thing to do," Ross said, shaking the papers. "Marcia, you never should have brought these home."

"Why not?" she wanted to know.

Ross sighed, looking up. "Because if Uncle Joe finds them missing, what do you suppose he'll do?"

Chapter Fifteen

We were to find out within minutes. The doorbell rang, its faint echo reaching us, closeted away in the library.

"Now, who do you suppose that could be?" Marcia asked, turning her chair to face the door. She bit her lip and stared straight ahead, trying hard to hear the conversation taking place at her front door.

The murmur of voices teased my ear. I couldn't make out a word, but could only distinguish between Dolores's high-pitched voice and a lower one that I guessed belonged to a man. Anxiously, I glanced at Ross. The intensity of the look he returned made it plain he suspected trouble.

As several sets of footsteps drew nearer, Ross shuffled the telltale papers into a pile and thrust them at me, jerking his head in the direction of my purse. My hands were trembling as I fumbled with the catch on the bag. Rolling the papers into a tube, I pushed them into the depths of my purse and hastily shoved the bag under my chair. I had just straightened up when I heard Marcia gasp.

In the doorway stood Joe Whitson and his balding blond henchman, Bernie Keeler. Whitson's white hair seemed to stand on end. His cheeks were stained bright red with an emotion I hoped wasn't rage. His hands were balled into fists at his side. In contrast, Bernie looked ill at ease. He stood behind Joe, peering over his shoulder at us.

There was an instant of stunned silence as we all examined one another. I saw Ross reach out to Marcia, placing his hand on her shoulder.

Joe broke the tension, taking two strides into the center of the library. An ugly smile twisted his face. "Well, isn't this a tender scene?" he drawled sarcastically, his eyes burning into Ross and Marcia. "I never would have guessed I'd find you here," he said to Ross, shaking his head and forming his words carefully. "This comes as such a shock!" He put one hand over his heart.

"Cut the theatrics, Joe," Ross directed, rising to his feet. "What do you want?"

Joe didn't answer the question. Instead, he shook a finger in Ross's face. "You know, you have an attitude problem. I don't like your tone."

"State your business, Joe."

Marcia grasped the wheels on her chair and slowly backed up until she was next to me. I got the feeling she was clearing the space for a duel. Not a welcome image.

"My business, Ross, is the mill. *My* business," he emphasized. "Not yours." Joe's eyes focused on me, narrowing. "And certainly not hers!"

I gulped, smiled, and said, "Good evening, Mr. Whitson." *Two can play at this sarcasm game,* I thought.

"Yeah, well, you'll see how good it is when you're out of a job," he threatened. "I'll take that rag you work for to court and bankrupt it!" he shouted. "Spreading vicious lies about the mill, all that garbage about pollution — just who do you think you are?" He tried to advance on me, but Ross blocked his path.

I clasped my hands tightly together in my lap over my notebook. My fight-or-flight instinct was operating at full speed and I wanted to either punch the old conniver in the nose or run all the way home. Instead, struggling, I sat very still, crossing my ankles in an attempt to hide the purse tucked beneath the chair. "I'm a reporter, Mr. Whitson. I report facts. All the facts, whether you like it or not." My voice came out smooth and flat, devoid of all emotion. Good.

"Facts!" He spit out the word, turning

away from me in disgust.

"Which facts would you like to discuss first, Uncle Joe?" Marcia asked. "The false toxic-emission statistics or the bank balance of the Environmental Fund?" She held herself rigid, braced for an explosion.

"This is all your fault!" Whitson went back to Ross. "You're just like your father. Always stirring things up."

"Don't bring my father into this." Ross took a step forward, anger barely held in check. He jerked a hand to ward off Bernie, who had made a hesitant move forward. "You don't have to worry, Bernie. I won't hurt him. He'll need to be healthy for the trial."

"Trial?"

"Of course. You can't avoid the long arm of the law, Joe. You've bought yourself plenty of jail time," Ross stated.

"You're all crazy! You can't prove a thing! I've done nothing wrong." Joe crossed the room in several nervous paces. I'd seen this man several times in the past — schmoozing with state officials at fund-raisers, presenting checks at charity functions — always the dignified picture of authority. Now, his charm deserted him, his composure cracked and fell away.

"If we can't prove these accusations, why did you try to hurt Anthony?" I asked. "He's been a loyal employee for decades and you nearly killed him!" I knew I couldn't be sure Joe Whitson had been behind the attack on the informant, but my gut told me he was. Frank always told me to go with my gut reaction, and this time, it paid off.

"Oh, that was just to scare him. To shut him up," Joe dismissed the incident. "If he hadn't fallen into the ditch, he would have gotten a few bruises. That's all."

His words — so cold and calculating — chilled me. I looked at Marcia for her reaction and was not surprised to see astonishment on her face. She'd taken plenty of blows to her world of illusions in the past few days and here was another.

"Uncle Joe!" Her voice was raspy. She moved across the room to where he stood near the fireplace, and she looked up at him in shock. "I thought Tony was your friend. Is this how you treat your friends? How can you? How can you live with all these lies?"

The color in Joe's cheeks faded and his angry scowl slipped away. It was like watching a storm-tossed lake settle down, the white-caps dying in foam. He reached out a hand gently and stroked her shiny hair. "Marcia, I never meant for you to be involved," he said quietly. "No one was supposed to know."

"But why did you do it? The mill turns a

good profit. You collect a decent salary. Why?"

His hand fell away. "All those pollution controls would have cost the mill a fortune," he said. "It was bad enough we had to purchase the equipment. If we'd ever actually installed it, costs would have rocketed and cut into the profits."

"And reduced your personal cash flow," Ross put in. "You wouldn't have been able to put as much money into your Environmental Fund."

Joe whirled around to confront Ross. "That fund was established by a bonafide committee."

"With members who bark and chirp," I interjected.

Joe looked from one determined face to another. We sat in stony, expectant silence.

"We can prove it all," Ross said. "We've got the documents."

"You took them," Joe addressed Marcia, and she nodded. "My secretary said you'd been in. It didn't take me long to realize why. That's why I came here. To get them back."

"It's too late," Marcia lied. "They're already in the hands of the authorities."

"No, that isn't true," Joe rushed on. "It can't be. You wouldn't do that to me." He spread his hands in appeal. "Look, surely we can work something out." He smiled, looking like the con man he was. "There's plenty of money to go around. I already give a little stipend to a few men at the mill."

"The statistics collectors?" I asked.

"Yeah, yeah. But there's enough left for all of us. Ross, you could use a little extra, right? Marcia?" He grinned at me. "I know you could. They don't pay reporters much these days." His chuckle, meant to be good-natured, rang false and grating.

"I can't believe you said that!" Ross exclaimed. "You just don't understand. You honestly think you can buy us off?"

"Oh, come off it, Ross. Don't act like such a do-gooder." Joe bristled.

"It's not an act!" Marcia defended her brother. "He's a decent human being, unlike you. I'm so disappointed." She looked down at her hands, knotted in her lap.

I could tell her words stung. Joe opened his mouth, then shut it again. Finally, he said, "Well, that's too bad. If you all want to be happy in the poorhouse, be my guest. But I'm not going with you and I'm not going to jail."

My moment had arrived. I cleared my throat. "I'm afraid you will," I declared. Raising my voice, I added, "Isn't that right, Chief Hately?"

There was a commotion in the doorway. A

few seconds later, Oakwood's chief of police strode into the room, flanked by two uniformed officers. "Sure looks that way, Lauren," the chief said, advancing on Joe. "Men, read him his rights."

Chapter Sixteen

I took a sip of hot, strong coffee. Looking around the kitchen table at several anxious faces, I laughed.

"All right, Lauren," Ross began in his no-nonsense, lawyer voice. "Marcia and I have been very patient with you. We waited while the police arrested Joe and Bernie. We waited while the chief had a little chat with you. And we waited while your coffee brewed. But now" — he put his hands on my shoulders, feigning anger — "we want an explanation!"

Ross, Marcia, and I had joined Dolores in the kitchen after the police had left. Dolores, who had watched the drama unfold from the hallway, greeted us all with hugs of reassurance and congratulations on a job well done.

"I never did like that man," she confessed, offering us cookies she had made just that afternoon. "He always was kind of shifty." The two of us exchanged a look and she nodded, a secretive smile twitching at her lips.

"Remember the other day when I said we should go to the police and you thought we should wait?" I asked Ross, reaching for a cookie.

"Y-yes," he drew the word out, one eyebrow sliding upward.

"Well, I didn't listen to you. I went with my instinct and I went to the cops. Chief Hately and I had a long talk. I showed him the evidence we'd gotten from the mill and told him about our meeting with Marcia here tonight." I turned to Marcia. "I hope you don't mind."

She shook her head. "Not at all. Please continue."

"I told the chief we were planning to stop at the station after our meeting, but that I would feel better if we could all see him as soon as possible. All the intrigue we've experienced lately made me edgy." I shrugged. "If anything bad was going to happen, I wanted Oakwood's finest close at hand. You can't get much closer than right in the next room!"

"But how did they get in? The doorbell only rang once and that was Uncle Joe," Marcia said.

Dolores spoke up. "I let them in the back door, dear. Lauren called me this afternoon and we arranged it between us. She knew as well as I did that both of you would be too stubborn to call the police until you were

203

good and ready. Lauren didn't think we should wait that long. And she was right." The older woman leaned over and patted my hand, giving me a charming smile.

"Uncle Joe showing up came as a surprise, then?" Ross asked.

"I'll say!" I stated. "But actually a very welcome one. The police heard his confession to both the pollution charge and the embezzling. Plus, I have it all on tape!" My trusty recorder had run throughout the ordeal, making it easy for me to lift direct quotes for my next newspaper article. I would get the front page for this one, I thought.

"What will happen to Joe, Ross?" Dolores questioned.

"The feds will be filing charges against him for the mill violations," he said. "That plus the theft should guarantee he goes to jail. It will leave the mill in a bit of a lurch, I'm afraid." He looked at Marcia. "What will you do?"

His sister's strong personality asserted itself. "The Board will meet and appoint a new officer, I imagine. An interim one, at any rate, until we can reorganize."

I ate another cookie, thinking about the future of the mill. "Well, if anyone can straighten out the situation, you can," I told her sincerely. "I'm sure you'll pull the company together in no time. You've proven you are levelheaded in a crisis."

"Thanks for the vote of confidence." Marcia turned to Ross, poking him with her elbow. "This girl's a terrific judge of character. You'd better not let her get away."

Dolores joined in, teasing the two of us until my face blushed red and Ross stammered denials.

"I don't plan to let her get away, you two busybodies," he said in his defense.

"And I don't plan to go!" I put in, linking my arm through Ross's.

"I think I hear wedding bells!" Dolores sang.

"And I think I see the headline," Marcia said with a grin.

Ross picked up the cue. "I'll bet I know who will write that story."

"*Reporter Weds Alderman,*" I cried, making quotation marks with my fingers. I kissed Ross's cheek and added the line, "By *Lauren Whitson.*"

Oh, Mom, I thought as Ross gave me a squeeze, *wait till you hear about this!*

The employees of Thorndike Press hope you have enjoyed this Large Print book. All our Large Print titles are designed for easy reading, and all our books are made to last. Other Thorndike Press Large Print books are available at your library, through selected bookstores, or directly from the publishers.

For more information about titles, please call:

(800) 257-5157

To share your comments, please write:

Publisher
Thorndike Press
P.O. Box 159
Thorndike, Maine 04986